# THE EMERALD GARDEN

by
## Jerry Hill

The Emerald Garden
© Copyright 2017 by Jerry Hill

To my beautiful wife Alisa, for all your love and support. I love you. You rock!

To Gerrit, Lexi, and Hayden, I could not be more proud of you guys. I love you.

To Lizzy, the only French girl with four legs I have ever loved.

To the GREAT science fiction writer, Nick Cole. Your encouragement and support has been overwhelming. Thank you.

# CHAPTER
1

All I can think about is getting out of this place. I have to escape. This cannot possibly be the end. I am so tired of hurting. So tired of feeling the burning in my stomach. The chemotherapy has ruined me. I cannot take another pill. My skin feels like it is on fire. I have not had a good night's sleep in months. The constant poking and prodding is driving me crazy. I have to escape this prison cell of a hospital. I have been drifting in and out of consciousness. When I am present is the worst. The constant questions of "how are you feeling"? The never-ending taking of my vital signs. Sleep is impossible. The nurses never seem to leave my room. The machines I am hooked up to are constantly beeping and sometimes alarms are going off. That usually triggers another nurse entering my room to mess with the buttons so the alarm will turn off. When I finally try to sleep the cycle seems to repeat itself, and I slowly realize that sleep and rest will not take place in this hospital. When I try to nod off, the noise and busyness of my particular wing of the hospital are too much to bear. It seems like there is always an emergency, and there is always an announcement going through the in-room speakers asking for a doctor or a nurse to come to a particular room. My pain is at an all-time high, and the patients around me keep me awake with their constant groaning. I have tried the methadone. I have tried the oxycodone. I have taken more tramadol than most humans can bare, and I have worn out the drip button that releases the morphine into my body. This just seems like a terrible nightmare. It's like when you used to dream about trying to run from a bad guy in a dream and you simply can't make your feet run, and the bad guy is catching up, and you keep trying to run. Then you finally wake up in a panic. That is what this seems like. I am in extreme pain. This has to stop. I have to escape this bad dream. I need to wake up. This can't be real. Please let me wake up. Please wake up!

As I sat up in my hospital bed, I began to take off the wires that entangled me. The wires that had held me hostage for so long. First went the wire that attached itself to my index finger. That was the wire that monitored my pulse. Next I pulled out the drip that had been in my arm feeding me and hydrating me. I then pulled the blood pressure cuff off my arm to the screeching of the velcro. After being in a hospital bed for so long, I just wanted to feel fresh and alive again. So, the first thing I wanted to do was change out of this ridiculous dress they give every hospital patient. You know the one. It's this skimpy smock-type dress that ties in the back. We used to wear them in kindergarten when it was our day to paint pictures. You would put that on to prevent paint from getting on your clothes. I have no idea why hospitals have chosen that as the patient uniform, but it needed to go. I swung my legs over the side of the bed and reached for the pinkish plastic tub they'd put my clothes into when this nightmare began. I then took off the gown and put on my jeans, polo shirt, and tennis shoes. I reached for my wallet and watch, and headed for the bathroom in my room. I grabbed a washcloth and washed my face and arms, then brushed my teeth and hair. It felt so good to finally be leaving this prison cell. My body felt great. The pain was gone. My skin felt normal, and I had such clarity of thought. After getting dressed, I went over to the table in my room and poured myself a glass of water, drinking it as I stared out the window and watched the world go by several floors below. I felt so good. I opened the door of my room and went past the nurses' station as they were working at the same crazy fast pace they had been since I'd arrived. As I pressed the elevator button for down and waited, all I could think about was how great I felt. I could not wait to feel the cool Lower Manhattan air. As I stepped out of the elevator and into the hospital lobby, the place was really busy. Nobody noticed me because they had so many different things going on all at once. I stopped off at the vending machine in the lobby to pick up an ice-cold Coke. It tasted so sweet and refreshing. I felt normal again for the first time in a long time. I really wanted something to eat as well. I thought about heading downstairs to the hospital cafeteria, but then I got a whiff of some of the food that was being prepared, and realized fresh air would be preferable.

I walked out the front door of the hospital onto William Street. I looked into the blue sky and there was not a cloud to be found. The sun was out and it seemed like the perfect summer day. The sun began to warm my face, and it reminded me of just how great it was to be outside again. The fresh air was fantastic, as I took a deep breath and it filled my lungs. It's amazing how much I took fresh air for granted. The air was cool but not cold, and it just felt great all over my body. The city was alive with people hustling from one place to another, the cab drivers going crazy with their horns, and you could feel the energy. People ran from place to place and everyone seemed late for a meeting of some kind. However, for me it was like a new start. I felt amazing. No pain, no stress, and nowhere to be. As I walked down William Street I was filled for the first time with such wonderment. I am not sure why, but given what I had just been through, I was not asking too many questions. I felt great, and was on my way home. I headed to the Fulton Street Station to catch the next train. As I was walking down the sidewalk, I happened to notice the Federal Reserve Bank of New York. It was tall and majestic as it rose into the sky. It looked like a cool stone castle from another era. People were hustling in and out of the building at a rapid pace. It looked like a busy place. I couldn't help but think, that all the money in that bank could not make me feel any better than I do right now. As I continued down the sidewalk I saw the subway station ahead. I stopped off for a moment to hear a young street musician play his guitar. He was playing folk music. Most of the people were in too big of a hurry to stop and listen. I just sat there on one of the benches and listened to him play for a few minutes. I was really enjoying this day. The perfect weather always seemed to bring out the best of the city. Sitting on the bench listening to the music, I noticed just how many birds were also singing in the trees above the musician. I really enjoyed my personal guitar concert. As I got up to continue on my journey, I reached into my wallet and dropped a hundred dollar bill into his guitar case. I then started back down the sidewalk headed for the train. I entered the station, and headed for the automated ticket machine. I got my ticket, and descended the stairs to the platform. As I was waiting for my train, I noticed for the first time the mosaic tile on the wall of the station. It was this cool brown and green tile with the letter "F" in the wall. The letter stood for the obvious: Fulton Street Station. I wondered why this was the first time I'd noticed that. I have been in this station many times before, and never saw that. I guess that's what happens when you have nothing to do, and all day to get there. As I was waiting for the train, the platform began to get crowded. New York is such a great city. The people are so diverse, and watching them makes for great entertainment. This is a city where you can have a woman dressed in a four-thousand dollar business suit, talking with a janitor who just got off the night shift and is heading home. The train finally arrived after a short delay, and I quickly boarded and took a seat. The subway was always interesting. Whenever you boarded it and sat down, you could not get past the idea that the entire thing was filled with germs. The seats are plastic, and usually some faded color of orange or yellow. The advertisements are everywhere on the walls. They want to sell you on the latest watch or television show. Most of the time graffiti is painted everywhere, and for reasons I still have not figured out. On this particular day, the train was filled with so many different people all checking their watches and cell phones every two seconds. On a train this large it was weird to not see one person who was not glued to their phone. Well, that's not entirely true if you count the drunk man passed out, taking up three seats to work off whatever he had for lunch. Most of the people on board today seemed late and completely stressed out. I just sat there in my seat, happy to be alive and feeling great. The train rocked back and forth as we sped through the tunnels of New York, and would come to screeching halts as we entered the next station. As the train came to a stop, the busy and stressed out people would pile out, and a brand new group of the same would board the train. This pattern had repeated itself until I came to the last stop. It was weird because I was the last person on the train. The drunk man even found the motivation to get up and exit the train two stops ago. I stepped off the train onto the platform, and headed for the stairs. I always wondered why they never put escalators in the subway stations that would take a passenger from the platform to the street. The stairs always seemed like they never ended. However, that did not bother me today. I had plenty of energy and took the stairs like an athlete training for a big race.

When I got to the exit doors of the station and opened them, I noticed something strange. I was expecting to see the hustle and bustle of the city. I was expecting to see the hot dog vendors, newspaper stands, and dozens of taxis waiting for customers. I was also expecting to see my favorite Italian restaurant in New York: Paulie Gee's. I wanted to go there and fill the hole in my stomach with one of their great slices of pizza. I love that place, and their pizza is the best. I thought I would see the sidewalks alive with men and women hurrying to their next appointment of the day. The same type of busyness I had seen when I boarded the subway back at Fulton Street. The crazy type of energy that has made New York such a wonderful place to live. Cars honking, people yelling, and the smell of restaurants preparing for dinner. The sun going down on another day in the concrete jungle. The city life that I had grown to love. The same life that most people around the country find repulsive, but native New Yorkers absolutely love. However, what I saw next was shocking.

But then again, seeing your whole life flash before your eyes is probably something that would be shocking for anyone, even though you lived it all, one day at a time. Every moment of it was more important than I'd ever imagined.

# CHAPTER
## 2

It was the perfect Summer morning to go fishing. My dad had the day off work and school was on Summer Break. The sun was out and the temperature was to reach into the low 80's today. A perfect day to be out on the water. Growing up, my dad has always taken me fishing. I always enjoyed those days. The actual catching of the fish has never really been an issue. Me getting to spend time with my dad was the most fun part of those fishing trips. My dad had rented a little dingy from Smitty's and we were heading for deep water on Jamaica Bay. This was our fishing hole. The bay is located between JFK Airport and the town of Far Rockaway. So, you get this great view of the city and the fun of watching jets take off while you fish for Striped Bass and Blues. The bay always seems like it is the perfect place to spend the day. The water is calm and it is the perfect escape for my dad and his stressful work life. My mom always packs us the perfect lunch and puts it in our old red Igloo cooler. She makes us peanut butter and jelly sandwiches, and always adds in chips, fruit, and a couple of Cokes. It always makes for a fun day. I think one of the very first things my dad ever taught me to do was tie a Dropper Loop knot and attach a hook with a five-ounce weight. He always stressed the importance of using a Bucktail Jig if we are fishing for Striped Bass. If we decided we wanted to catch some Blues it would be a shiny Spoons lure. I learned quite a bit about fishing when I went with my dad. If we ever caught anything, my mom was a good sport and would clean and cook the fish for dinner. She would also act like it was the best fish she had ever tasted. My dad and I would look at each other and just smile. My mom was the best.

For as long as I can remember, when I was fishing with my dad, he would always tell me about a common friend he and and my mom shared. The name of this man was William Biddle. My dad would always launch into long stories about how Mr. Biddle had taught him different life lessons. He would sometimes go into great detail to explain the character of this man as well. My dad would tell me about how William Biddle came along at the perfect time in his life. It was at a time when my dad really needed a male role model and mentor. When I asked my dad to describe him he said, "Mr. Biddle was a man who was of average height and weight, and always dressed in a suit and tie, but never acted pretentious. He was a man who wore clothes that were a little too big, but they were always clean and presentable." My dad just guessed that he did not have much money, but was raised to always look sharp. I asked my dad what Mr. Biddle did for a living. He said, "Mr. Biddle ran the local travel agency and was a friend to anyone willing to spend a few minutes with him in conversation." I asked what area of travel Mr. Biddle specialized in. My dad said, "He is a man you go to when you have decided that your travel itinerary is not what you thought it would be, then he tells you about a new itinerary." I asked my dad what he gives you for a new itinerary? My dad went on to explain, "He gives you a gold box that has a red ribbon on it, and in the box is a key that changes everything." My dad went on to describe him as, "the most humble and good natured man he had ever met." He said Mr. Biddle would come over to the house and they would talk for hours at a time and sometimes Mr. Biddle would never get a word in edge wise. My dad said it never seemed to bother Mr. Biddle when the night came to an end. Dad told me, "Mr. Biddle was not the type of man that drew attention to himself, and never pushed his agenda on another person unless you specifically asked him a question." Dad went on to say, "He would simply say his goodbye and smile from ear to ear as he left our apartment." My dad was so fond of him. I asked my dad where Mr. Biddle worked, and did he have a good business? My dad replied, "He has an office in Midtown Manhattan, and I have never been there when it was not crowded." My dad told me, "You will need to meet him and get the gift he has personally given to me and your mother." The gift box with the key, I asked? My dad said, "Yep, that's the one, and you will never regret it."

My name is Dexter Hightower, and I grew up in Far Rockaway, New York, a neighborhood in the borough of Queens. It was a great place to grow up and I happened to be born into a wonderful family. I may have the most perfect mother and father ever born. I hit the genetic lottery. I currently attend middle school here in Queens right off Mott Avenue. My school is an easy walk from our apartment on Cornaga Avenue. In the mornings I walk to school with some of my friends in the apartment complex. It's a friendly neighborhood with hard-working middle-class people. Everyone seems to look out for each other, and respect and honor the authorities. It's a clean town with modest homes and apartments, and the residents are gold. This town was the perfect place to grow up. We had the corner grocery store where everyone knew each other, and you would get to catch up with your neighbors when you ran into them at the store. It was always a great place for my mom to go and catch up on the latest town gossip. I enjoyed going to the store with her because it usually led to me begging for a candy bar and her rolling her eyes as she complied. It was also a town where we had a great ice cream parlor, cleaners, insurance agent, and barber. I loved going to the barber shop with my dad. This was a place where the men could be men. They loved my dad there since he was a man's man, and always had me in tow. We generally got our hair cut there twice a month, and I always looked forward to that visit. This town was great.

My father's name is Robert Hightower. He is a New York City policeman. He's stationed out of the 115th precinct right here in Queens. His station is located on Northern Boulevard in the Jackson Heights neighborhood. You can't miss the building. It's made up of all red brick and looks like a fortress. The police station is always flying the American flag, and I have never been there when it was not really busy. My dad loved taking me into the station and showing me off to all his co-workers. He was always bragging about how I could hit and throw a baseball. He would always tell them how I was the future of the New York Mets. They would needle him and everyone would have a good laugh. Those people were family to my dad. They loved him and he loved them and serving his community.

My father is a hard-working man who loves his family and God. He is a sergeant in the NYPD and is absolutely dedicated to his job. He has been eligible for promotion many times and always turns them down. He has never been interested in a desk job and being part of the managerial politics that come with a promotion. He loves being around the other cops out on the street. He is known as a no-nonsense man who serves his community with pride and dignity. He is loved by his fellow cops and many of the residents of Queens. My dad has been there for the people many times over the years. He has taken down robbers as well as delivered babies. He has also driven home more than his fair share of drunken teenagers. My dad always felt like it was better to take those kids home to their parents than to jail. He said the sentence from mom and dad would be far worse than anything he could deliver. He has been on the job for thirty years. He has also been an elder in the local First Baptist Church for the past twenty-five years. The congregation at church loves my dad. They tell me often of his wisdom and love for the people of our church. They are grateful he has the time to serve the congregation. My dad often gets calls from the pastor asking him to go and visit someone from the congregation in the hospital or their home. So, my dad always goes and meets with them and will often pray for them. He has always modeled for me what it means to work hard, love your wife, serve your community, love your son, and cherish your country and God. He is just a solid man. He loves to spend time with me and his schedule allows him to do that on a frequent basis. He enjoys taking me fishing and to Mets games. He is a huge baseball fan, so as a result the game was gifted to me at birth. My mother loves to show me the photo she took of me when we left the hospital together after my birth. The picture is of my father holding me in one of those hospital blankets all wrapped up with a small Mets hat on my head! So, when I say I was born into baseball, you understand. It was my dad who taught me how to play baseball. He bought me a glove and a bat at a very young age. During the summer he would take me to the local park and throw me batting practice, hitting me ground balls until it was impossible to see the ball. He always told me I would become a great baseball player if I stuck with the game and practiced often.

My mother's name is Norma Hightower. In many ways she has always been the glue that held our family together. She is the most loving mother any son could ever dream of having. She is an elementary school teacher right here in Queens. Her school is located on Wanser Avenue and is a simple walk from our apartment. My mom is really loved by the school she works for as well as the children. She is the type of teacher that spends a tremendous amount of her own money on supplies for her class so the children she is teaching will have a better experience and education. I don't believe in the thirty-five years she has been teaching, she has ever missed a back-to-school night or an open house. Twice a day she meets her children at the door to give them hugs and reassure them that they are loved. It happens when the kids arrive at school in the morning and when the afternoon bell rings to go home. Several times over the course of my mom's career she has been honored by the school district as an outstanding teacher. The district has told her many times that they are inundated in the summer with phone calls from parents who want their children in her class. This always makes her feel special, and she should feel special because she is really good at what she does for a living. She loves being a teacher, and the kids, parents, and staff see that on display each and every day. She has a tremendous work ethic as well.

My mom has always been the type of lady who will go and visit a sick neighbor, or reach out to someone who has just experienced a death in the family. Her presence just seems to make others calm down and really feel loved. I have been told by others that my mom always seems to know just what to say to others to make them feel good. She has always been the type of mother who can crack the whip when it comes time for homework to be done, and also be the first one to mention the Mets game is coming on television. She has always done her best to instill in me the character qualities she believes are the most important: honesty, integrity, and love for others as well as God. She has modeled that to me my entire life. She is also a woman who has gone through extreme hardship. My mom has known great pain in her life. That may be one of the reasons she is able to reach out to others so successfully. Five years before I was born my mother was pregnant with her first child. She made it to the eighth month of her pregnancy before things went tragically wrong. My sister Rebecca had decided she was going to be born early. The complications came when she was entangled by her umbilical cord that caused the oxygen to be cut off from her brain, and she died in the hospital shortly after being born. The doctors had done their best to try and keep her alive, but in the end she was gone. My mom and dad told me it took years to figure out how to keep living each day after the death of Rebecca. They were devastated and completely drained of energy and life. My mom had a tremendous amount of guilt. That led to long bouts of depression and remorse. She blamed herself at times, and would go through days where she did nothing but cry. My mom told me she was devastated. She told me that what had kept her going during the dark times was her faith in God. She said she was relying on the promises she had read in the Bible, and she knew God was a gentleman and would keep them. My parents knew they would never get over her death, and it was going to take time to figure out how to live life again. That is one of the many daily burdens they have learned to carry. To this day they are grateful for one of the pediatric nurses that was working with them that day. She was experienced and sensitive enough to ask my parents if she could take a picture of them with Rebecca. My parents with tears in their eyes agreed, and that framed picture hanging on the wall of our living room, is our most prized possession.

I find it interesting how life is as fragile as a piece of fine china. People have the ability to endure extreme heartache at times, and can be broken by simple spoken words. Life has a way of throwing all of us curveballs, and sometimes we will take a third strike, and have to head back to the dugout to regroup for the next at bat. There are very few things in this life we can choose, but we can wake up every day and choose our attitude. We can choose to be good neighbors, and we can choose to be loving people. We can allow our circumstances to define us, or we can rise above those circumstances that tend to bring us down. We can choose to be helpful, and we can choose to have good manners. We can choose to be kind, and we can choose to care about others. We all have choices to make in this life. My hope is that each day we wake up, we choose wisely. Life is precious.

# CHAPTER
## 3

Tomorrow is the big day. Each year for as long as I can remember, my mom and dad have saved their money so my dad could take me to the Mets game on Opening Day. This always occurred in early April and often allowed me to miss school. As painful as that was for my schoolteacher mom to bear, she was always so excited for me. This also meant that the night before the big game, it was next to impossible to fall asleep. That night at the dinner table we would all discuss the starting lineups of both teams and run through the rosters like we were about to be called to the field to manage the team. Usually by the time I went off to bed, my head was swimming in statistics and potential lineup cards. I always loved how excited both my mom and dad would get about Opening Day. I knew that was special, because talking to my friends I always saw a different side. They would tell me that their mom and dad really didn't like sports, and some of my friends had never been to a Major League Baseball game. So, I knew my mom and dad were special, and I loved the fact that they were always as excited as I was for the season to start.

The morning would eventually arrive and my mom always made us a big breakfast before we headed off to the ballpark. She would be up before anyone, and you could smell the bacon and eggs throughout the apartment. The smell of sizzling bacon was the best alarm clock ever invented. Since it was always a special occasion, she would also make her homemade cinnamon buns. They were amazing, and the white frosting she made for the top of them was better than ice cream. My dad and I would arrive at the table at the same time. Our arrival was always preceded by my mom calling out that the "restaurant was now open for business."

Opening Day was usually a one o'clock start time. This day for me was just as exciting as Christmas. My dad and I would always make sure we arrived at Roosevelt Avenue in plenty of time to see the gates open and watch batting practice. The greatest structure ever built by man was on Roosevelt Avenue in Queens. It was Shea Stadium where my beloved Mets played baseball.

On the way to the stadium my dad would always launch into the same stories about the 1969 "Miracle Mets". I was too young to remember when they'd beat the heavily favored Baltimore Orioles, but through my father I was certain to never forget. As often as I had heard all his stories I never grew sick of them. I loved to hear the passion in his voice as he got excited about baseball. He would remind me of the great pitchers the Mets had back then. He would go on and on about Tom Seaver, Nolan Ryan, and Al Jackson. The way he talked about players like Bud Harrelson, Jerry Grote, and Ken Boswell, the casual listener would swear they were his children. My dad loved the Mets, and he loved America's favorite pastime.

As we arrived at the park you could feel the excitement in the air. Opening Day represented a clean slate. Baseball fans around the world had high hopes for their favorite team on Opening Day. Every fan to ever watch the game believed their team could win the World Series on Opening Day. Nobody ever showed up at the ballpark thinking their team would lose. It was a day of high hopes, and big dreams. The Boys of Summer were back from Spring Training, and they were ready to play for keeps. You could feel the excitement in the air, and people had smiles on their faces.

My Mets were one of the first Major League Baseball expansion teams. They were founded in 1962. This was a result of the Benedict Arnold- Brooklyn Dodgers leaving town with the Judas Iscariot- New York Giants in hot pursuit. Then out of some weird love affair, the decision was made to make the Mets' uniform colors partly Dodger blue and partly Giant orange. I guess to terrorize me and every other kid from Queens for the rest of our natural life. However, we loved our Mets. They were our team and we were so proud of them. Every boy from Queens grew up loving the Mets, and pretending to be their favorite player whenever a stick ball game broke out in the streets. We always fought over who was the greatest Met of all time, and which one playing today was currently the best. It usually never got solved, and ended up with several verbal fights as well as choice words being exchanged. However, one thing was clear: we loved the Mets and baseball.

Arriving early to watch batting practice was always a great highlight. It really gave you the opportunity to see these guys hit and field. I was always amazed how hard they hit the ball, and how effortlessly they swung the bat. These guys were like finely-tuned machines. I also liked batting practice since you could move around the park freely, and try to get a foul ball or a home run. The ushers never seemed to mind the herd of kids going crazy jumping over chairs, and each other, to get the coveted leather prize. It was also fun to bring a ball and pen and see if you could get any of the players to sign it for you. The smell of popcorn and hotdogs in the air was intoxicating. There is nothing quite like the crack of a wooden bat as it connects with a fastball. I would always make my way over to the bullpen to see the starting pitcher warm up for the game. You could hear the pounding of the catcher's mitt anywhere in the stadium. These guys threw the baseball hard, and they were playing for keeps. As you watch the game it is three to four hours of pure joy, and a feeling of euphoria comes over you. It always feels awesome when a new baseball season begins. Opening Day is unbelievable! This day should be a National Holiday.

On the way back home from the ballpark my dad began to tell me again some of the stories of how his friend William Biddle had influenced his life. I asked my dad how did Mr. Biddle influence you? My dad said, "In so many ways. First, he was a very calming influence in my life during a time when I thought the world was spinning out of control." I asked my dad what was out of control in your life? He said, "I was struggling with so many things. I had grown up in a family of alcoholics, and that had led to me being physically abused as a boy." I asked him what his father used to do to him. He replied, "He would get drunk and stumble home late at night, then wake me up and tell me to get out of bed, and tell me how bad I had been. Then he'd take off his belt and beat me with it until my mother finally jumped in to stop him." My dad continued, "I would go to bed with welts on my arms, legs, and back. They would eventually become bruises, and I would have to explain what happened when my friends would see me in the locker room before gym class. I ran out of excuses over time, and they stopped asking. It was humiliating. They had figured out what was going on at my house." I did not know what to say next. I was in shock. My dad had never told me that before. I can't even imagine having to go through that as a kid, especially by someone who is supposed to protect and love you! After I had gained my composure, I asked my dad after all that ugliness, how could he have turned out to be such a great father? My dad looked at me and said, "Thank you, son. I could never have become the man I am today without the help of Mr. Biddle. He has completely changed me from the inside out." My dad went on to say, "He taught me about the value of honesty, integrity, and self-control. He taught me how to be a man and take responsibility for my actions, and to never blame others for my behavior." He continued, "Mr. Biddle showed me what hope looked like, and he gave me a purpose for my life." My dad went on to say, "He told me how I did not have to feel alone and ashamed about what had taken place in my life. That it was not my fault, and that God loved me very much." I asked my dad if that was the time he had accepted the gift box from Mr. Biddle? My dad said, "Yes, that was the time. However, understand that once you accept the gift, it takes a lifetime to figure out how to live with the gift." I asked him what he meant by that? He replied, "The gift is wonderful, but this life is filled with all sorts of evil, and you still have to find a way to navigate the waters of this life with love and grace, and not give in to all the things that tempt you each day." I asked him where he kept his key He told me, "I keep it on the top of my dresser, so I can be reminded each day about how that gift has changed my life."

My father was a deeply religious man and had been taking me to church since I was born. Everyone at church knew me because of my dad being an elder in the church for so many years. I was dedicated to the Lord in that church as a baby. My mom and dad had told me about that day several times. So, I grew up in the church, and always had a healthy respect for Christians. I just never considered myself one. I believed in God, but that may have been out of respect for my mom and dad. They were such good people, it was impossible not to notice. I have just never felt the need to be religious. I don't hate God, and I would never consider myself an atheist. If you were to ask me about evolution, I would tell you it sounded more difficult to believe in than Christianity. I may be looking through rose-colored glasses, but my life was awesome, and I could not imagine ever being less excited about life than I am today.

After we arrived back home, I had to spend the next couple of hours giving my mom a recap of each inning. I am convinced she could have done without it, but I think she enjoyed my enthusiasm. She made us a great dinner, and it was the perfect ending to a wonderful day. As I placed my head on my pillow, all I could think about was how awesome Opening Day had been. I love baseball.

The one thing I learned today, is just how complicated life can be at times. It reminds me of trying to put together a thousand piece jigsaw puzzle, and the manufacturer left out four of the key pieces. People are hard to figure out at times. We have so many leaders around the world threatening one country or another, and people groups rising up in different countries to protest their governments' abuses. At times we just throw our hands up in the air, and wonder how any of this can possibly make sense. I wonder what would happen if the entire world took just one day to go to the ballpark and watch a baseball game? Everybody on the same day. The worst thing that could take place, would be some folks might get sunburned for the day, and others might eat too many dogs. However, nobody would leave grumpy and mad at life. They would leave happy, and telling stories about the game they just saw take place. That would be a perfect day.

# CHAPTER
# 4

On Sunday nights we went to church. It was something we did just about every Sunday night I can remember. I usually enjoyed Sunday night service more than Sunday morning, because it was less formal and a whole lot less time consuming. The great thing about Sunday night service is we would get to go out to dinner when the service ended. This particular Sunday night our church had decided to honor the officers of the New York City Police Department's 115th Precinct. That is the precinct my father works out of, and they had the best results of any precinct in New York City. They have had the record for the fifth straight year. So, the pastor and elders of our church had decided to honor the officers in a formal ceremony that night at our church.

It was always fun to see my dad in his dress uniform. He looks so official and he always looks proud to represent the finest police department in the world. His jacket was immaculate. It was adorned with gold buttons, and on both sleeves he had the patches that signify the Police Department City of New York, and the scales of justice. His badge was polished to perfection with his name tag below, and above the badge he had three additional accommodations. The first one represented Honorable Mention. This was awarded to him for extraordinary bravery performed in the line of duty. Below that was another commendation. This one was for-Community Service. This was awarded for an act which demonstrates devotion to community service. The final commendation was for Commendation-Integrity. This was awarded for grave personal danger in the performance of duty. He also wore a silver 115 on his collar to represent his precinct. Down the left sleeve of his jacket were hash marks signifying five years of service for each hash mark. His black shoes were so polished you could see your reflection in them. He looked amazing. My mom wore a special dress she had made just for the occasion and I wore my best clothes. This was a special night and we wanted it to be perfect for my dad and his fellow officers. They were a tight family, and this was their night to be honored for their service to our community, and the bravery each of them exhibited every day they wore the uniform.

When we arrived at the church it was already almost completely filled to capacity with the different officers, their families, the current church families, and various city officials. This was turning out to be a very big deal to so many people. The pastor started the night out with a heartfelt welcome and opening prayer. The various city politicians got up one by one and gave their respective speeches, and the night closed with my father leading the congregation in a hymn. I have never seen my dad look any more proud than he did this night, and the smile on my mom's face seemed like it would be there for a couple of weeks. After the service was over, everyone was invited into the courtyard for coffee and cookies. During that time of fellowship you could tell the officers were having a great time. They introduced their spouses and significant others to everyone. The children looked bored and ready to leave, but it was the officers' night to shine.

We finally arrived at my favorite part of the Sunday night service, deciding where we will go for dinner. On our way to the car, the decision was made to go to the best hamburger place in the city. The name of the restaurant was Mike's Burgers. It was home to my dad's favorite burger, the pastrami burger. It was an easy decision since this was my dad's favorite place to eat dinner. As we drove down Beach Channel Drive, all we could talk about was how great the service had turned out. My dad was really proud of his pastor and the church for stepping up and organizing the night. My mom talked about how all the women she'd spoken with loved the service, and were grateful for the church. Then, all I remember is getting to the intersection at Mott Avenue, when everything went black.

I was told several days later, when I awakened in the hospital, that we had been in a horrible car accident. Apparently when we had arrived at the intersection of Beach Channel

Drive and Mott Avenue, there had been a tremendous crash. A drunk driver had ran a red light and smashed into our car head on. As we waited to turn left, he had drifted into our lane after running the light and smashed into us while traveling about seventy miles per hour. He left no skid marks, which indicated he never touched his brakes before impact. I had been in a medical induced coma for the past couple of days to try and bring stability to my condition. I had several internal injuries as well as swelling of my brain. My right arm and leg had been broken as well. I was sitting in the back seat right behind my dad who was driving. My mom had been in the passenger seat next to my dad. As I asked for my mom and dad, I was told to wait for a couple of minutes while the nurse left the hospital room. The nurse returned and I was greeting by some other nurses and our pastor. The pastor informed me that my mom and dad had been killed in the crash. I literally thought they were playing a joke on me. I asked them again, and they told me I was the only survivor. The driver of the other car was also killed. I had no idea how to react. I was so sore, and my head was spinning. I felt like I was going to vomit. I began to cry uncontrollably. It was too much to deal with. I was hoping it was a dream. How could this have happened? We had just gone to church, and were on our way to dinner. No way my mom and dad were not coming back for me. They would never have just left me in the hospital by myself. What would I do? Where would I live? How could I go on living? They could not possibly be dead. This has to be a mistake. As I continued to cry, all I could feel was the pastor gently holding my hand. I was still hoping it was all a dream.

As I ponder life, I am amazed at how quickly a person's circumstances can change. One day you're fine, and the next day your whole life can be turned upside down like a bag of marbles. Everything can seem in order, and in its place, and the next thing you know the marbles are all over the floor. Then you are scrambling to pick them up as they are going in all directions. You just want them to be back in the bag all neat and together. Unfortunately, life does not always cooperate. It can be messy. Circumstances can change in the blink of an eye. Life has a way of throwing you a fastball that is high and tight, and backing you off the plate.

# CHAPTER
## 5

The Holy Sisters of the Faith Orphanage, located on East Houston Street in Lower Manhattan, has become my home for the next five years. The orphanage is located just on the other side of the Williamsburg Bridge. When I turn eighteen, I will then be released as a ward of the state to pursue other arrangements.

My new home is run like a military operation. It is home to about seventy boys who vary in age from ten to seventeen. In my bedroom there are twenty beds. The beds are really like military cots and they are pretty close to each other. When I first arrived I could not believe so many boys could actually fit in the same room. I also realized very quickly that when it is time to get some sleep, that is not so easy with that many guys in one room. There seems to always be snoring, coughing, or just general restlessness. Sleeping was difficult at first. I share a common bathroom and shower with those same nineteen roommates. I have learned to get up early so I don't get caught having to wait around for a shower and a toilet. We also have a study hall in the house to make sure we have a place to do our homework after school. That also took some getting used to since I usually did my homework at the dining room table. Not in a room with seventy boys. At meal times we gather around large tables that seat about twelve boys per table. Every boy is assigned different chores that need to get done each day. I have been assigned the job of washing dishes after dinner along with sweeping the hallways at night. I am not the only boy who has to wash dishes. There is a crew of about ten kids. On the weekends we all have the job of cleaning the bathrooms and showers. It's amazing the mess seventy boys can make in a day. The food seems to be pretty simple at times. They serve us the cheap kinds of food. We have lots of rice, chicken, and hamburger meat. Most of the time there are a few vegetables, but we never have soft drinks or dessert. My guess is most of the food is donated by various groups around town. It takes quite a few people to run the kitchen, and feed that many kids. There are no snacks, and the kitchen is off limits during the day and night. So, you'd better eat what you're served, because there will be no other food offered. That has taken some time to get used to as well. I have always been a light eater, but would snack constantly during the day and night. The whole thing has been a tremendous adjustment. I am still not sure my stomach is used to the change. I have lost weight since living here.

The orphanage is run by a local Roman Catholic Church and is staffed by the same church. Most of the people on staff are nuns and look at this orphanage as their ministry. They have to be really strict to keep seventy boys all in line and following the amazing amount of rules they have written down and told me dozens of times. I am also responsible to know and recite those rules whenever I am asked by one of the nuns or the main priest. I am not sure it is even possible to keep all the rules. There is not a day that goes by that I am not lectured extensively for violating one or several of these rules. I used to think I was a pretty good person, until I found myself a resident of this place. Now not a week goes by that I don't think about leaving this place the day I turn eighteen. Sometimes I just lay back in bed at night and wonder why none of my relatives stepped up during this crisis to allow me to live with them. I guess it was just asking too much. On those nights I will often think of my mom and dad, and my old friends in Queens. I have a new school now and a new neighborhood. A new home and new roommates. Nothing is the same. I am lonely most of the time. I try not to think about it too often since it usually results in me crying myself to sleep. In this place that is not that uncommon. Most of the boys are just surviving.

I think it may be the personal things that I miss the most. Like being tucked into bed at night by my mom. Having my dad tell me about his day. Looking at the way my mom and dad smiled at each other. Having dinner together as a family. I remember when it was my birthday how my mom would always decorate the house, and make a chocolate birthday cake. She and my dad had this special way of making me feel so loved and wanted. I really miss that feeling. I really miss the little things. I really miss them. I often find myself in the middle of class just closing my eyes and trying to remember them and the fun we used to have as a family. How I loved going to baseball games with my dad. How Opening Day was like a national holiday. Usually about the time I realize I'm daydreaming in class again, and that these are simply just memories, the tears begin to flow. I have gotten way better at hiding them and concealing my feelings. Living in an orphanage with seventy boys will definitely have this effect on a person. You really can't allow yourself to show any weakness. So, I try not to think too often about mom and dad. The one thing I've noticed is how lonely I am at times. I'm surrounded by all these boys, and yet I still feel alone. That has been particularly difficult. I never realized how much I relied on my mom and dad, and my friends as well, to keep me entertained and functioning. I guess that's normal. The problem is, I really feel like I'm on my own without a family to fall back on for love and support.

A family is probably one of the most underrated entities on planet earth. We live in a society that really stresses independence and the individual. A family is something that is completely different from independence. The family is a group of individuals that do life together. They support one another. They love one another. They show care and concern for the other members of the family. They are there for each other when things go wrong. You can talk to them in confidence, knowing it will stay in the circle of people who love you. They're also there to celebrate victories together. They're there to tell you they're happy with your success, and proud of your accomplishments. A family is a tight-knit group of supporters who love being together. That is what I had. But I'm now like a starting pitcher throwing a perfect game. That pitcher arrives in the dugout at the end of each inning, and no one will talk to him. He sits on the far end of the bench, lost in his own thoughts. No one wants to talk to him, because they might jinx the perfect game. I don't like being the starting pitcher.

# CHAPTER
## 6

The passing of time is always interesting to me. My time in the orphanage has passed pretty quickly. Days have become weeks, weeks have become months, and months have become a couple years. As I have pondered my time here I am always left with the feeling of being alone, sad, and completely empty. The nuns have treated me fine, but I feel like I am just trying to survive this nightmare. I really have become angry at my mom and dad. I feel completely ripped off, and I have no idea how to make things right, or even how not to feel this way. I have found myself thinking, and looking at every situation in the negative. I don't ever remember doing that before the accident. Since the accident, I look at the negative in everything. I guess I would have to say that I have become bitter and jaded. I really have no idea how to look at my situation any differently. My memories come flooding back without the slightest care who is around me at the time, and most of the time I simply cannot control their return. It's like your crazy uncle who just shows up on your doorstep and announces he is staying for the weekend. It's random and usually ends in me feeling more depressed and lonely.

Today at the orphanage we are celebrating all the birthdays that have taken place for the past four months. That's what they do here. I guess it's a whole lot less expensive doing this in bulk rather than as individuals. So, today I get a birthday party along with twenty-two other guys who live here. This usually involves a cake and some hot dogs and chips. Nobody ever gets a present, because that would cost too much. The birthday parties are fun, and we have a great time teasing each other that day. It is by far the best day we have at the orphanage. It's a day you can almost forget where you have come from, and where you are now. You realize the pain you're feeling is mutual. It's seen on the faces of those guys around you, and together you can make each other forget for a few hours. So, the parties always provide for a little bit of an escape from the realities of the world. The nuns always do their best to make things nice. However, at the end of the day, it's still not your family. I am not really close to anyone here at the orphanage. That has been difficult. It really leads to feeling lonely. I am not sure if it is just me, or it really is that hard to make new friends.

I did something today that I have tried to resist since the day I arrived here at the orphanage. I walked out into the front yard of the house and looked across the East River.

From my front yard in Lower Manhattan you can see across the river right into Jamaica Bay. The very spot my dad used to take me fishing on my birthday. I have only done this a couple times in the past. I really didn't want to do it today, but with the celebration of my birthday, the temptation was too great to resist. The memories of my dad and mom came flooding in like a broken dam. My dad and I used to have so much fun going fishing out on that bay. I can remember us playing so many different games when the fishing was slow. We used to guess what plane would be next to take off from JFK. We would literally keep score and play until someone would reach twenty, and was declared the winner. I knew every airline that flew out of that airport. Those were such happy times and great days. It's really difficult to get my mind around the thought that they are dead, and will never be coming back to take me home.

I stood out in that yard, until I thought it was impossible to cry another tear. Just when I thought I was done crying another torrent of tears would overcome me. The memories were amazing. They were so real. In those few minutes, I felt really free. I felt like I had a family again, and my mom and dad would be here any minute. I guess I am just an emotional mess. I feel sad. I feel lonely. I feel abandoned. I feel unwanted. Most of the time I just try not to remember. It's really the memories that bring the tears. It's also the memories that bring the sense of being alone. I really need to try and not remember. I used my shirt to wipe all the tears off my face, and went back inside the house. The party ended shortly after I returned, and everyone went to their room or to the study hall areas, to begin their homework.

As I laid in my cot thinking about the day, Sister Mary came to tell me I had a visitor in the living room. I could not imagine who was coming to visit me. A few of my dad's friends would show up randomly to check in on me. But those times were few and far between. They were busy guys with families and children of their own. It usually would lead to an awkward conversation, mainly since I really never knew them. I did appreciate what they were doing. I knew they were checking in on me to honor my father, and the friendship he had with them. They were all good men and I respected them all. However, being told I had a visitor was exciting. It was especially exciting since today was my birthday party. My mind raced to try and figure out who would be calling on me today. As I walked through the house, I could not come up with any names. However, I was still excited.

I walked into the living room to find an older man dressed in a suit and tie. His suit was neatly pressed, his tie was perfect, and his shoes looked nice, but not fancy. He was a slender man, but very fit. His hair was short and black with slight greying around the temples. He was clean cut, and shaven. He stood to his feet when I walked into the room, and introduced himself as William Biddle. He asked me, "Have you ever heard about me"? "Do you know who I am?" I told him, " My father and mother spoke about you all the time." He had a warm smile and a relaxed way about him. He was one of those types of people that allowed you to feel comfortable in his presence. You really got the idea he thought you were way more important than he was, and so he just allowed you to talk most of the time. I told him, " My dad would tell me all about you when I was a kid." I went on to say, "Whenever my dad and I went fishing or to a baseball game, inevitability the conversation turned to you. My dad would always tell me how grateful he was that you had become part of his life." He seemed to enjoy the fact that I was telling him all about how my parents appreciated him. I went on to tell him, "My mom also spoke about how fond of you she had become. She always gave you credit for changing her life." Mr. Biddle said, "First of all I wanted to wish you a happy birthday." He then said, "I am sorry that you lost your mom and dad in that car accident. I was there at the hospital when you all arrived by ambulance. I was also at the cemetery that day, for the joint funeral of your mom and dad." I asked him, "What was the funeral like?" He said, "It was the perfect day. The sun was shining, and the sky was a perfect color of blue. Your mom and dad had been escorted to the cemetery by a large procession of New York City Police vehicles and officers. There were hundreds of officers at the gravesite." Mr. Biddle continued, "Your pastor gave a great message, and the church choir led us in several songs. The NYPD had an Honor Guard give them a twenty-one-gun salute. Both your dad and mom had their caskets draped by the American flag. After the service was over, we went back to the church for a luncheon. There must have been five-hundred people at the luncheon. It was a beautiful service, for two of the sweetest people I have ever met." I asked him, "Did any of my friends show up?" He said, "Yes, they all did, and all your teachers and Little League friends. In fact, every one of your Little League teammates wore their uniforms. It was really cool. You would have been proud of them."

I soon began to realize that William Biddle was a master at getting me to share my feelings, and talk to him. It was just easy to talk to him. He's a great listener. He eventually asked me, "Tell me how you're doing with losing your parents, and now having to live in an orphanage for the past couple of years?" I said, "It's been a difficult adjustment. I have been really lonely, and often find myself going through depression. At times I feel like I am in a dark tunnel and there is no way out." He said, "Please share with me how you have become angry." I replied, "I am angry at times with my parents for leaving me behind to fend for myself. I also feel like I have been robbed of everything good in my life." I went on to explain, "I have never been a huge fan of God. However, I have always admired my mom and dad's faith, but never found it necessary for me. Yes, I grew up going to church each Sunday, because that was always important to my parents. I genuinely admired that about them as well." However, I went on to tell him, " If God was real, how could he have ever allowed my parents to be taken from me? And if God was so loving, how could he have allowed me to wind up being raised by people I don't know, in a place I don't want to be? How could a loving and gracious God do that to me? I simply cannot believe in a God who allows me to get so ripped off, and does nothing about it."

Mr. Biddle looked at me with with compassion in his face and voice and said, "I can completely understand why you are feeling angry, depressed, and lonely over your situation. I also can understand why you would be feeling angry with God, and why you believe God has let you down. Please know that these feelings are normal. Your doubting God is normal. Please also know that God is not offended by you. He understands the pain you have gone through, and he loves you very much." Mr. Biddle was giving me permission to feel upset. He went on to tell me, "God is not someone who is waiting to hit you over the head with a baseball bat every time you do something wrong. God truly cares about you, and wants you to have a life that is fulfilling, by using the gifts he has given you to their full potential." He went on to explain, "God is not going to run and hide because you are mad at him. God understands your anger and knows it sometimes just takes time to work through bad situations and events that effect everyone's life. Please understand that it was not God's will that your parents were killed by a drunk driver. There is the presence of evil in this world that affects both good people, and bad people, in negative ways. This has a tremendous effect on everyone who is living, and walking around today. That is what makes this life so difficult to figure out at times."

Mr. Biddle went on to say, "Dexter, I can help you with your current itinerary. I am sure your parents told you about me being a travel agent." I said, "Yes, they did." Then he said, "Then let me help you. You don't need to necessarily come to my travel office in Midtown Manhattan like your parents have done in the past. I can help you right now if you'd like. I have a gift for you, if you're willing to accept the fact that your current itinerary is flawed, and you need a new one. Are you willing to receive my gift? I looked at him with a lump in my throat and said, "Yes, I am." Mr. Biddle then reached for his briefcase that was beside the chair he was sitting on, and pulled out my gift. He said, "Here is your gift." He handed me a beautiful gold box that had a red ribbon on it. I asked him, "Is this the same gift you had given my mom and dad?" He replied, "Yes, it is, the very same gift. Please open it up." I then untied the red ribbon, and looked into the box. I found a very interesting key in the box. The key was not your average house key. It was also not like any car key I had ever seen. The key was like one of those old skeleton keys that would open the door to some medieval knight's castle. You know the one you always see in the movies. I asked Mr. Biddle, "What does this key do?" He said, "The holder of this key will find love, joy, peace, long-suffering, kindness, goodness, faithfulness, gentleness, and self-control. You will have to work at all of these, but your life will be forever changed. It does take a lifetime of practice, but these characteristics are yours forever. Please know that I will be praying for you."

I thanked Mr. Biddle for the visit, and walked him to the door. I went back to my room, and laid on my bed, just staring at the key. I could not escape the thought of having just received the same key my mom and dad had told me about, so many times in the past.

Hope is an amazing gift. We can give hope to so many people by just saying a kind word. We can give hope to people that have virtually nothing, by simply being kind to them. Hope has built great buildings and bridges. Hope has also built great kingdoms and kings. Hope has allowed single mothers, working two jobs, to come home and love their children. Hope has the power to allow us to rise above the worst circumstances, and soar like eagles. Hope has the power to change the world. May we never lose hope.

# CHAPTER
# 7

I came to the realization now that I was in high school, that not everything in my life had completely blown up in my face. This year I'm going to be a senior in high school. When it came to high school, I hit the lottery. I've been attending Grover Cleveland High School on East 2nd Avenue. This is located on the Upper East Side. This school is amazing! I have no idea how I got into this school, but it has been great. Each day I get on the subway at East Houston Street, and travel past the Empire State Building, then Times Square, then the Central Park Zoo. I then get off the train at the 96 Street Station, on the Upper East Side. Then it is just a short walk to school. This is where the people with the big bucks live and their kids go to school. This is the place where it's safe to go to school, and walk the streets. I was going to school in the land of Range Rovers and limousines. That was cool. The school was really nice, and the classrooms looked brand new. The athletic fields and stadiums were the best I had ever seen. The school had poured a ton of money into their sports programs.

The school academically has been a challenge. The orphanage has not been the greatest place to grow up academically. It's always difficult to study because of the noise, and you simply don't have access to your mom or dad for help on some of the basic things in school. So, as a result I have to make notes and remember to ask the teachers the next day, if I remember. That can place a long delay on writing a paper or getting to the bottom of a math equation. However, there is little doubt that my teachers are helpful, and want me to succeed academically. This high school is definitely a great prep school for college. Many of the seniors that are graduating have their sights set on the big Ivy League schools. They also have the grades and SAT scores to match. This is a school that wants you to go to college. They tell you that at the beginning of your freshman year. The parents of the kids that attend are all highly educated. As a result, those same parents are very successful.

The one thing I have become very good at is baseball. I've had the opportunity to play on one of the best fields in America since I arrived at Grover Cleveland High School. The facility was amazing and the coaching was even better. They really spared no expense at this school when it came to academics and athletics. They take both very seriously, and when you participate in sports you'd better take it seriously as well. They tell you straight up, second place is just the first loser.

I've really taken off physically between my sophomore and junior years of high school. Then add onto that, a school that has a weight and conditioning coach, and I've gotten pretty big. I am now six-feet, four-inches tall, and weigh two-hundred and twenty pounds. It is really difficult to get any kind of a fastball by me and if you throw me a curveball, it will be landing over the outfield wall. My coach told me I have one of the best arms he has ever seen on a shortstop. He said there is no doubt I will be drafted by a Major League Baseball team after my senior season. When my coach told me that, I was stunned, excited, and sad all in the span of about five minutes. I really had no idea I was going to be good enough to play pro baseball. The thought of that made my heart jump. However, sadness completely came over me at the end. All I could think about was growing up going to Mets games with my mom and dad, and how much they would have loved to see me play baseball. They would have completely rearranged their schedules to come watch me play my high school games. My dad would have been so proud of me. He would have bragged about me to his buddies at the station and they would have come to my games as well. My mom would have cheered me on from the stands, like so many of my teammates' mothers do for them. I had not cried in a while, but that day I just sat in the visitor's dugout as the tears flowed. I literally tried to stop them and it was impossible. I can't for the life of me figure out why it's so difficult for me to feel happy or proud about something I have accomplished. In the end I always wind up thinking about my mom and dad. Those thoughts generally turn into tears, anger, and deep depression. I simply cannot shake this pattern. I think what I struggle with most is the feeling of being lonely. It's the feeling that I am doing this all on my own. I don't have parents to share the victories with, and the great memories. So, I am really struggling with being alone.

Since it was my senior year, I decided maybe a girlfriend would help me escape the pit I had fallen into emotionally. I thought if I had someone I could care about, then maybe I could shake the feeling of being alone. So, I decided to date a girl I had met last year in my science class. She was a nice girl from a wealthy family on the Upper East Side. She was absolutely beautiful inside and out. I think the most difficult thing I have experienced in high school was showing her where I live. She had really pressed me to go and see my house. So, I took her to the orphanage. I honestly think she was shocked. She had no idea that kids could even grow up in these places. She really seemed sorry for me. I think the worst part about her visit was the guilty feeling she had because she was from a wealthy family. She would take me over to her house and her parents would really bend over backwards to make me feel welcome. I am sure it was because she had told them the whole story of going to see me at the orphanage, and how I lost my parents. They had a beautiful home. It was about fifteen-thousand square feet, and had ten bedrooms and fifteen bathrooms. It was awesome. This place was a mansion.

She was a nice girl, but I could tell this was not going to work. She was always pressing me about my past, and it was simply too painful to continue to talk about. I always found it difficult to stay close to anybody. So, when it came time to share about my past, it was tough. How can you continue to explain how loneliness has overwhelmed you, and maintain a relationship? It's not very easy, but I'll try.

My girlfriend's name is Kelly Anne Simpson. She's six feet tall, with blonde hair and blue eyes. She's a senior this year, just like me. She enjoys riding horses and going to movies. She is currently carrying a 4.0 GPA, and wants to attend Harvard. Her goal is to become a pediatric surgeon. She comes from a family that has given her the same love and support my mom and dad had given me. She's a very sweet girl, who's also involved in the community. She volunteers at the local soup kitchen, and tutors young grade school kids on the weekdays. She's a perfect girl.

Tonight was her birthday, so we decided to celebrate by going out to dinner. I asked her, "Where do you want to go for dinner?" She said, "It doesn't matter to me, as long as we can be together." So, we drove to a restaurant that makes great hamburgers. When we arrived, we were seated immediately. I asked Kelly, "Tell me your fondest memory of growing up in Manhattan." She went on to explain, "When I was a little girl, my dad would always take me to the zoo. We would go on Saturdays and spend all day looking at the animals, and just talking." She continued, "I just enjoyed getting to spend time with my dad. He was gone most days and night working in his law firm, so I did not have the chance to spend a lot of time with him. I always knew he loved me, but spending time with him was always precious." She asked me, "Tell me about your dad." I went on to tell her all about my dad, and his job as a policeman. I told her about the times we would spend out on the water fishing, and the fun we had going to baseball games. I also told her about how my dad used to coach my Little League teams. Then she asked me, "Tell me about your mom." I told her how my mom taught school, and all her kids loved her. I also told her about all the times my mom would volunteer to be the Team Mom for Little League. I then went on to tell her about how my mom often took the time to visit people who were sick, or had just experienced a death in the family. She then asked me, "Were my parents religious people?" I said, "Yes, they were. However, they would have objected to the term, "religious". They preferred the term, "Christian". She then went on to tell me how her parents had raised her in the Presbyterian church. She said they would go to church a couple times a month. I asked her, "Do you believe in God?" She replied, "Yes, I do. I don't think you can look at all the beauty this earth has to offer, and somehow think God does not exist." I told her I agreed with that thought. It was about that time that our waitress showed up with dinner. We enjoyed our dinner for a while, and then she began to ask me more questions. She asked, "Why do you seem to feel alone most of the time?" I replied, "I think it is because my family was taken from me at a very young age, and I had to grow up too fast without their support."

She said, "Do you have any friends at the orphanage?" I said, "Not really. It has been difficult for me to make friends since the death of my mom and dad." She went on to say, "Have you ever thought that you're afraid to make friends?" I asked her what she meant by that statement. She replied, "You may not want to get too close to people, because maybe in the back of your mind, you feel they will abandon you. Like you feel your mom and dad have done, and you don't want that pain again in your life." I thought about those words for a while, then replied, "You may have a valid point." I then went on to tell her about our family friend, Mr. Biddle. I told her all about how my mom and dad were changed after visiting him, and receiving the gift. I explained that I too had asked and received the same gift. She asked, "What was the gift?" I pulled the key from my pocket, and placed it on the table. She picked the key up, and studied it like there was a test on it in the morning. Then she said, "That is really cool. Do you keep it with you wherever you travel?" I said, "Yes, I do. It is my lucky key, and it is on me wherever I travel." I then told her that my dad kept his key on his dresser to remind him of the promise, and my mom kept her key in her jewelry box, on the bathroom sink. That was so she could see it each day. However, I kept my key with me at all times. She thought that was great.

My senior season in baseball was becoming a huge success. I was having a great year and our team was headed to the state championship. I had been awarded the league MVP. It was a great year. I was hitting .520, with 12 home runs, and 45

RBIs. I did not make a error all year at shortstop. My coach said it was the finest year of any player he's ever coached. So, he said to get ready because in June, Major League Baseball will have the draft. This is where all the professional baseball teams gather and choose the different players they would like to draft, and have sign a professional baseball contract. This is the first step in becoming a professional baseball player. I was excited about that prospect, but really needed to focus on the job at hand. That was competing in the State Championship Game. Winning that game was all that mattered at the moment. I knew it would mean the world to my teammates, and the school. So, we had a couple of weeks to get ready. Our opponents were going to be the Indians from Ketcham High School in Wappingers Falls, New York. This team had a great record this season, and some outstanding players. We will have our hand full if we are to return champions.

The day finally arrived for the State Championship. The game was going to be held at our high school since we had the best record. We arrived at the ballpark early for batting practice. All high school games were seven innings. Our ballpark was really large. It seated about four-thousand people, and had a large grass area in left and right field just past the outfield fence. That area could easily hold another two thousand people. The field was large. Down the left field line it was 320 feet, to center it was 400 feet, and to right field it measured 340 feet. Both the left field and right field power alleys measured 360 feet. So, there was plenty of room to run. The foul areas along both the third base and first base sides were spacious, as well as behind home plate. This was a true pitcher's park.

The umpires called everyone out of the dugouts for the National Anthem. As we lined up along the third base line, it was impossible not to notice all the people who had showed up for the game. The stands were completely full and you could barely see any grass with the enormous crowd sitting on the slopes beyond the outfield walls. When the anthem was over it was time to play ball. This was the game we'd worked so hard to get to all season. The time had finally arrived, and it was time to stand up and deliver a championship.

Since we were the home team, we had to take the field first. Dan Engel was our starting pitcher. He'd had a great year. His record was 9-0. This kid threw a 90 MPH fastball with the best slider I have seen in high school. He was our ace, and he was healthy and ready to deal. They sent three batters to the plate in the first inning, and we got them out in order. One strike out and two ground ball outs. The final ground ball was hit to me up the middle, and when I gloved the ball, I was so pumped I thought I might throw the ball into the stands. Our first baseman made a great catch and saved me. It was our turn to hit. I was hitting in the third position. The first guy up walked. The next guy up tried to sacrifice bunt him to second, and popped the ball up. On the first pitch to me, my coach put on the hit and run. The pitcher threw me a fast ball, and I hit it off the wall in deep center field for a double. The runner scored and we were up 1-0. The next two batters struck out.

In the top of the second inning, they got a runner to second, on a hit into the gap. The next two guys struck out. The next batter hit a weak pop fly that dropped just over our second baseman's head, and the run scored. The next guy up grounded out to me. The score was tied 1-1. As we came to bat in the bottom of the second inning, our leadoff man got aboard on a single up the middle. He then stole second base, and was driven in with a sharp single to right field. The next batters went quietly. The score was now 2-1.

To start the third inning, we had the bottom of their lineup. Dan was now fully engaged, and throwing really hard. He struck the first man out, and the second batter grounded weakly to third, for the second out. The number nine hitter was coming up to bat. This kid looked like he was scared to death. The first pitch was a fastball that hit the outside of the plate, and this kid stepped to the ball, and drove it over the right field wall. So much for being scared. The next guy hit an easy fly ball to left field, for the final out. The game was tied 2-2. We were now coming to bat. Our number nine batter was coming up. He grounded to short for the first out. The next guy up hit a bullet by the third baseman, and wound up with a standup double. Our next batter hit a weak grounder to second, for the second out. The runner advanced to third. I came to bat, and was sitting on a curveball. The first two pitches were fastball strikes. I was still waiting for the curve, and it finally came on the 0-2 count. I waited on the pitch, and hit it over the left field wall, into a mass of screaming fans that had risen to their feet to receive the ball. As I rounded third base, I saw Kelly for the first time, and she was on her feet going crazy. Our next hitter then took a fastball over the center field wall. It may have been the farthest homer I have ever seen in high school. The next batter grounded out to the shortstop, for the final out. The score was now 5-2, the good guys.

The fourth inning started with some fireworks, and they scored a couple of runs early. Our left fielder had butchered a fly ball, and the next batter had hit a curveball over the right field wall. We changed pitchers, and brought in our closer. Walt Macduff was a big left-handed kid, who just looked intimidating. He threw hard, and would scream and yell at nobody in particular. To the other team, he just seemed crazy. He had great stuff, and retired the next three hitters for the last out. The score was now 5-4. We went quietly in the bottom half of the fourth inning. A little too quietly for our coach. He gave us a tongue lashing before we hit the field.

The first batter in the top of the fifth inning, got on with a drag bunt down the third base line. He was then sacrificed to second. The next hitter up struck out, for the second out. The next batter hit a weak line drive over my head, and the run scored. The final out was a pop fly to the catcher. The score was now tied 5-5. When we came up to hit, I think every guy knew we needed a run this inning. The momentum had really shifted since the third inning. Our leadoff man drove a ball into center field, and was on with a single. The next batter struck out looking. He had missed the sacrifice sign from the dugout. That sent our coach into outer space! I thought the man was going to have a stroke on the bench, he was so mad. The next hitter drove a ball into the gap in right center to score the runner. Our next two hitters grounded out, for the second and third outs of the inning. The score was now 6-5.

The sixth inning was really good for MacDuff. He came out firing strikes, and they really did not have an answer for this kid. He was throwing hard, screaming like a crazy man when he released every pitch, and they just kept hearing the umpire yell, "Strike three." Walt had struck out the side, and our fans could almost taste the win. They were going nuts. We came to bat in the bottom half of the sixth, and knew we needed some insurance. Our leadoff hitter was up, and hit a sharp line drive into center field for a single. The next batter up saw the sign, and executed the perfect sacrifice bunt. The runner advanced to second base. I came up and was guessing fastball. He threw me one and I lined the ball over the third baseman's head. The run scored, and I was on first base. Our next batter hit a weak grounder to short, and they turned a double play. The score was now 7-5, and we were pumped.

Walt continued on the mound for the start of the seventh inning. He was in the zone. He seemed to be throwing harder now, than when he first came into the game. Adrenaline has a way of getting ahold of you. It's the great thing about sports. The first batter came to the plate and hit a slow-rolling ground ball to second for the first out. At this point everyone in the ballpark is on their feet cheering like mad. The second batter hit a deep fly to center field, and our man in center ran it down for the second out. The next guy up took a third strike, to end the game. The celebration was on! Everyone ran to the pitcher's mound for a dog pile. The students started pouring onto the field, because we had just become State Champions!

Kelly and her parents had come onto the field to look for me. When they found me, we all embraced as they congratulated me. It was the perfect ending to my high school career.

Loneliness is a funny animal. At times you can be surrounded by teammates, screaming fans, and people who just want to hug you. Yet, you can feel completely alone. I can't really explain it. I just know that is how it works at times. Loneliness is usually the cousin to depression and sorrow. The interesting thing about loneliness, is it doesn't have to be the animal in the zoo you feed. Sure, you can feed it by not reaching out to others, and it will grow into a large beast. However, you can also be conscious that the animal is hungry, and try to starve it. You can do this by reaching out, and being friendly to others, and allowing them into your life. Sometimes, it just comes down to you. It always comes back to a person's willingness to become vulnerable. Maybe it's worth the risk. It has been said before, that you need to be friendly to have friends. That sounds about right. I also believe, you have to be ready to have friends.

# CHAPTER
## 8

It was June 9th and Major League Baseball had gathered in New York City for the draft. The draft was going to take place in one of the ballrooms at The Ritz-Carlton, Central Park. This was a beautiful hotel, located next to Madison Avenue, Radio City Music Hall, and The Museum of Modern Art. This hotel was really nice. The doormen always wore top hats, ties, and tails. The inside of the hotel was decorated in grand style. The floors were marble, and the furniture was beautiful. This was the perfect place to hold the draft.

The draft is held each year for Major League Baseball teams to select amateur players, for the purpose of offering them a professional contract. The players can be from a high school, college, or a tryout they may have attended. The order in which the team chose players was always a little random.

It depended on how well the team had done the previous year. However, this was also affected by teams that may have made a trade and given up a high draft pick to sweeten the deal. So, you could always wind up having really good teams picking first.

I was excited as well as many of my teammates. Today I would find out if I was good enough to play professional baseball. I sat with my coach and teammates in a room the school officials had set up for us to enjoy. The room was located above the baseball field, and had a great view of the school. The school officials had filled the room with all sorts of food and soft drinks for me and my teammates. As the draft was taking place, I must have checked my right front pocket a million times, to make sure my lucky key was still there. I eventually received a call from the Los Angeles Dodgers. They had drafted me in the twenty-second round. My teammates were really excited for me. I was excited as well. The Dodgers told me they had great hopes for me, and wanted me to report to their minor league facility in Glendale Arizona, within the next ten days. They went on to tell me it is a great facility just outside of Phoenix. They said they would fly me out in the next couple of days, and I would be housed in a local hotel. They would then figure out what minor league team to assign me to. In professional baseball, the Major League teams all have a farm system. This is a series of minor league teams that are located in different parts of the country. These teams are staffed by professional baseball players who have all signed contracts to play for that particular team. Those teams are ranked by the professional baseball clubs. Each team usually has a "Single A" team, a "Double A" team, and a "Triple A" team. The next step from AAA is the Major Leagues. So, the Dodgers were not sure at what level I would start. They told me that would all be worked out at their Spring Training Facility, in Glendale, Arizona. The minor league life is not easy. At the lower levels it always involves a lot of travel by bus, and not much money. So, it would be a big change from my current status. I would be playing baseball, and living with guys much older than myself. I would really be on my own, and need to provide for myself on very little money. I would need an apartment for the off-season, as well as a car. My head was spinning a little bit. What this all meant was, I needed to grow up even faster than I had been forced to when I lost my mom and dad. That was pretty intimidating. There was a lot to think about.

As I made my way back to the orphanage on the subway, I could not help but feel like I was not ready to play professional baseball. I had not been outside of New York, never lived on my own, had no idea how to cook, and never paid a bill. As I pondered all these things, I soon came to the realization that this might be coming at me too fast. Maybe I needed more time to mature in life. I had received several offers from universities that would allow me to play baseball at their school, and have it all paid for by them. This was certainly not a bad option. I enjoyed school, and had no problem studying and taking exams. I was already in the school mode. Many professional baseball players from the United States wind up going to college first, before they play professionally. The main reason for this is lack of maturity. When you attend a university, you also mature both mentally and physically. It also allows you to face better competition than high school, so you can become a more well-rounded player. This will often result in a player being drafted higher in the next draft, and receiving more money from the Major League team that drafts him. When I exited the train station I found myself staring across the East River again. This of course brought up memories of mom and dad. I could see Queens from the water's edge and really wished they were here to help me make this decision. I knew either way I was getting released from the orphanage. This had always been just a temporary home that I got to use. I really owned nothing, except the few items of clothes I kept in a cardboard box under my cot. So, a decision had to be made. I really wish I could have run this past my dad. I know he would have known what to do, and where to go. The advice that my parents always gave me was such a great help. I just wish I had that now. As I think back to when my mom and dad were alive, I really did take them for granted. Sure, I loved them, and appreciated the way I was raised. However, I never thought it would end so quickly. I never thought I would be unable to turn to them in high school for advice. I never thought I would have no more dinners with them. I never thought my mom wouldn't come into my room again to kiss me goodnight. I never thought my dad and I would never go fishing again. I wish I could have them back again. Just for a couple of days. I miss them.

When I walked through the front door of the orphanage, one of the nuns handed me a phone message. I had received a call from David Rolph, the legendary head baseball coach at the University of Southern California. He had been coaching there for the past ten years. In those ten years, his teams had won the National Championship five times. This man knew how to create great chemistry on a baseball team. He knew exactly who to ask to come and fill a vacant spot. This coach knew how to win baseball games. He had contacted me several times during the past two years, wanting me to come to USC on a full baseball scholarship. I guess I really never considered this, because I had always anticipated signing a professional contract. That was always my dream since Little League. I had really never considered college as a option. I think most kids only think about college when their parents talk to them. So, I don't think it was unusual that I hadn't considered going to college.

I decided to call Coach Rolph back. When he'd called me, he'd left his cell phone number as well as his home number. Since it was past dinner time, I decided to call his home. The phone was picked up by his wife, and she introduced herself as Anne. She told me to wait a moment and she would locate her husband. The coach came on the line, and I said, "Hi coach, this is Dexter Hightower." Coach Rolph said, "Dexter, thank you for returning my call. I wanted to congratulate you on being drafted by the Dodgers." I replied, "Thank you, but I'm not so sure I'll be accepting their offer to sign." He asked, "If you don't mind me asking, why are you hesitating?" I went on to explain all the reasons I could think of at that time. He said, "I fully understand your reasoning. I also understand how difficult this decision must be without being able to consult your parents. Please understand that I am here to help you. If you choose to come to USC, or choose another university, I will always be here to help you. You can bounce any thoughts or ideas off me, at anytime." I said, "Thank you. I was wondering what it would be like at USC." The coach responded, "When you come to USC, you are part of the Trojan Family. You will have the best education, and every resource will be at your fingertips to succeed. We want you to earn a degree, and have a great experience in the process. USC is a school that has some of the finest sports facilities in the country. We also have some of the best baseball coaches in the world. You will be taught things in the classroom, as well as on the field, that will challenge you immensely. You will be given every opportunity to be successful. Both as a student and an athlete. I think you should also look at coming to USC as a fresh start in life. I know your past has been painful, and maybe the change will bring a renewed sense of purpose." I replied, "I need a new sense of purpose. I've been struggling every day with loneliness, and at times severe depression. I can't seem to shake the feeling that I'm on my own. I feel I have no support system. I know that is not necessarily true, but I do have a deep sense of being alone." The coach went on to explain, "At USC you will make plenty of friends, and I will make sure you and I schedule frequent times to talk. At USC you will be following in the footsteps of some great baseball players. Many of our players have made it to the Major League level, and have enjoyed great careers. They also take the time to come back, and spend time helping and coaching the current players. I think with your talent, and our coaching staff, there is no reason why you can't become a first round draft choice after your junior year. That would completely change your life." I told him, "That is my goal. I want to become a professional baseball player. It's really the only thing I have ever wanted to do in life. I have never considered being anything else." He said, "Well, that opportunity is definitely a goal you can achieve. You just have to be willing to work hard, and take our instruction." I wound up speaking to Coach Rolph for a little over two hours. He was such a great listener, and I really felt like he had my best interest in mind. I told him at the end of our conversation, that I wanted to be a part of the Trojan Family. He was really excited, and promised me that it would be a great experience in my life. He said he would call back by the end of the week to help me make flight plans to Los Angeles. I thanked him again, and immediately called the scout for the Dodgers, to respectfully decline their offer. It had been a long day, and my bed never felt so good.

The next day I received a call from Kelly. She wanted to meet me, to discuss our future. I think we both understood what direction this was going to take. We agreed to meet at the 2nd Ave Deli on the Upper East Side. This deli had become a favorite place of mine. It was located between Lexington Ave. and 3rd Ave. They have the best pastrami and rye sandwich I have ever eaten. I also enjoy their matzo ball soup, and the white fish salad. The place is amazing. If you had just one more lunch to eat, you would be well advised to eat it at the 2nd Ave Deli.

I walked through the front door, and immediately spotted Kelly. She was sitting at a table in the back of the deli. As I approached the table, she saw me and stood up to greet me. I said, "Wow, you look as pretty as ever." She replied, "Thank you, you always seem to have the perfect words to make me feel great." I asked her if she had ordered, and she said she was waiting for me to arrive before she ordered. So, we both went to the counter to place our order. We then took our soft drinks back to our table to talk. I decided to kick off the conversation. I said, "I'm sure you've been thinking about our relationship as much as I have. I've decided to attend USC, and I leave in a couple of days for Los Angeles." She said, "Wow, when did you decide not to accept the Dodgers' offer?" I replied, "Just the other night, when I called the coach at USC, and we spoke for a couple of hours. I was doubting playing for the Dodgers right from the start. I was concerned that I would be having to survive on my own, with little to no money. I came to the realization that I have never had a job, paycheck, rent, or anything else. I guess I came to the conclusion, I am not ready to be an adult." She said, "I think it's a great idea. Placing myself in your shoes, I can say I would have made the same choice. I'm sure it was a difficult decision for you to make without the help of your mother and father. However, I think it is the right choice, and you are going to love college." I asked her, "When do you leave for Harvard?" She said, "I will be leaving in the next couple of weeks. The school has all the freshman arrive early for orientation, and to get situated in their new dorm room, before the returning students arrive. I am super excited to start the next chapter in my life. I hope you're excited to start the next chapter in your life as well." I said, "I am, but I am really hoping I can shake my feelings of loneliness." She replied, "I hope in some small way I've been able to help you. I know at times you've been distant. I also know how hard you've tried to be positive around me and my family. But, I know that you really still haven't made friends. I know you're still struggling." I said, "Yes, I'm still struggling, but you have been a tremendous gift. I've appreciated our time together, and how you and your parents have supported me. You guys have really blessed me, and made my life at the orphanage easier to take, because I knew I would see you at some point on any given week. That has really helped." She said, "I'm glad. I know we will not be continuing to date. However, I want you to know I think you're very special. I've enjoyed getting to know you. I know at some point our paths will cross again. I hope in some small way, I've made your life better. I know you've made mine better. I don't look at things the same way anymore. I used to take for granted things like my parents, and our home. Since I met you, I am a more grateful person. I have learned to appreciate everything I have been blessed with, and try not to act entitled. You have taught me so much." I replied, "I'm humbled by what you've shared. Please know you will always have a special place in my heart." She said, "By the way, I went to visit your friend Mr. Biddle. I went to his travel agency in Midtown, and received the gift." She then reached into her purse, and pulled out her key. She said she was so impressed by how the gift had changed me, she wanted it as well. She said she keeps her key in her purse. She wanted it to be with her at all times, like me. We finished our lunch, and gave each other a big hug. We agreed to call each other when we had a free moment.

I had to hop on the subway to get back to the orphanage, in Lower Manhattan. As I sat on the train, I was consumed with thoughts of Kelly and her family. They had really been a blessing in my life, and I was so glad I had taken the time to tell her about Mr. Biddle. She had such happiness on her face, when she reached into her purse and produced the key. I'm glad I met her, and had the courage to pursue a relationship. I think for the first time since my parents have passed away, I allowed myself to feel a little vulnerable. Our relationship really did improve my life at the orphanage. I'm not sure if we'll ever see each other again, but I'm grateful for our time together. I think I've become a better person as a result of her friendship, and I'll miss her and her parents.

The subway had arrived at my stop. I left the train and headed up the stairs to the exit. The walk down the sidewalk felt different for the first time. I think it may have been because I realized a new chapter in my life was about to begin. Everything I had grown used to in New York was about to change. In a way it represented a new start. In another way, it represented losing so much of what I have grown to love. It was sure going to be different in Los Angeles. I was looking forward to joining the Trojan Family.

I finally arrived at the orphanage, walked up the stairs, and into the house. As I entered the living room, I was greeted by Mr. Biddle. He said, "Hi Dexter, I hope you don't mind me dropping by to see you?" I said, "No, not at all. You are always welcome, and I consider you to be a part of my family." That brought a warm smile to his face. He said, "I was told you've decided not to sign with the Dodgers, and will attend USC in the fall." I replied, "That's true. I gave it a lot of thought, and decided I'm not experienced enough to start life on my own. I want to be able to continue improving as a baseball player, and enjoy the benefits of going to college." He said, "I think you have made the right choice, and I am proud of you. I know you will enjoy the college life, and gain some valuable wisdom from the experience. I have many friends in Los Angeles, and hopefully will be able to stop by, and watch one of your baseball games." I said, "That would be great. I am looking forward to my time at USC, and having you at one of my games would be a real treat." Mr. Biddle asked me, "Do you still have your key, and are you still battling loneliness?" I replied, "I keep my key in my right front pocket at all times. It has become my good luck charm. Yes, I am still battling depression and loneliness. I still have dreams of my parents. The dreams seem so real. I never want to wake up. I dream of fishing with my dad, and the times my mom and I would just sit around and talk. I love those dreams. However, when I wake up, I am always disappointed. They are gone, and I am still here. That's when I realize nothing is going to take my feelings of being alone away. I thought Kelly would, but I was wrong. I thought winning a state championship would do the trick. It didn't. I thought being drafted by the Los Angeles Dodgers would take my sadness and loneliness away. It didn't either. All of my success has not been able to do away with the feelings I'm dealing with on a regular basis. I thought all this success would bring happiness. It hasn't. I am completely at a loss for words. I am bewildered. Nothing in my life makes any sense." Mr. Biddle replied, "Dexter, I am glad you still have your key to happiness. I am also glad you keep it on you wherever you travel. Maybe the dreams you are having about your family, are a small gift to you from God. A way for you to remember the times when you were not alone. A little break from reality. The gift you have received from me is not a magic pill. The gift does not automatically take all the pressure of life away. The gift is not a quick fix. The gift is a reminder that this life is a process. There is no pill you can swallow, and never have problems. The problems in life will never go away while you are still walking this earth. The problems will change at times, but they will never simply vanish into thin air. The burdens of this life will be carried by everyone who lives on this planet. At times the names and faces change, but the problems never go away. Heartache, loneliness, depression, and sorrow are just some of the problems everyone must deal with at times. I know that television and advertisements paint a different picture. I know those mediums want us all to believe life is perfect. The problem comes when our life does not match up to the advertisement on television. We then think something is wrong with us. The truth is, this life is a battle. We will have times of great joy and happiness, and times of tremendous sadness." I then asked Mr. Biddle, "How do I make this life work?" He replied, "You have received the greatest gift imaginable. Please understand what you possess. Please also understand that the gift you received needs to be cherished, and shared with others. Like when you told Kelly to come and visit me. When you begin to see other people as being more valuable than you see yourself, you will begin to understand the gift a little bit more. This is a gift that needs to be experienced. This is a gift you need to practice life with, and allow others to see it in you. This gift is different than any other gift you have received. God has given you a sharp mind to excel in the classroom, and he has also given you tremendous athletic ability. Those gifts are great, but nothing compares to the gift you received from me. Be patient, and begin to understand the process of life. This is a journey, not a hundred-yard dash." I thanked Mr. Biddle for his wisdom and advice. I walked him to the door as we said goodbye to each other. I knew I would see him again soon. He really has an interesting way of showing up when I need him most. He is a great guy, and I am so glad my mom and dad spent so much time telling me about him. I can't wait to talk to him again.

As I begin to ponder the idea of a fresh start, it does seem to be a bit of an oxymoron. It sounds a little like, "jumbo shrimp". Or more like, "tragic comedy." I am not sure a fresh start actually is realistic. We all seem to be hardwired to remember our past successes and failures. So, we have made up a word for this occasion. We call it, "experience". Most employers want to hire people with experience. Most people really won't take advice from other people that don't have life experience. It's the experiences in this life, that allow us to be molded into the people we have become. That can be both positive and negative. When our experiences are negative, the trick is to not allow your experiences to define you. We all need to find ways to rise above the negative experiences, and embrace the positive. When our experiences are positive, we need to embrace and celebrate them. Our reactions to circumstances we don't control, will determine our effectiveness of reaching out and loving others. Love is an attractive and powerful force. Love never needs a fresh start. Love simply needs willing participants.

# CHAPTER
## 9

The morning had finally arrived for me to fly to Los Angeles and attend USC. It was really odd knowing I would not be returning to the orphanage again. The priest and the nuns met me in the living room, to wish me well. The priest asked if he could say a prayer for me. I told him that would be great. After the priest prayed, we all exchanged hugs. I saw a couple of the guys who I had shared a room with for the past several years, and they wished me well. It was a strange feeling as I left the orphanage in a cab headed for JFK. I had just spent the last six years of my life there, and that chapter was coming to a close. It was almost like I could feel myself growing up. It was strange. I really didn't make any friends at the orphanage, and my experience was not great. However, I really felt like I was going to miss that place. They had stepped up to support me in a time when I really needed the help.

They took me in and provided for me. No one else stepped up to do that for me. They fed me, clothed me, and sheltered me, when nobody else did. Sure, I didn't enjoy being there, but I had no other alternative. They stepped up, and came out of the bullpen to bring my life relief. I needed them, and they were there for me. I will never forget what they did for me.

When I arrived at the airport, it was really crowded. I made my way to the United Airlines counter, to get my boarding pass. Then it was time to wait in the security line. I made it through the line just in time. I heard over the loud speaker that my plane had started boarding. So, I got to my gate and boarded the plane to Los Angeles International Airport. I am always amazed at how small the seats are on a plane. There is absolutely no leg room for a guy like me. This was going to be a long flight, so I tried to get comfortable. I had a lot of time to think on the flight. I was excited about attending college. My great hope was it would allow me to make friends, and be happy. I know my mom and dad would have enjoyed the flight with me to Los Angeles, and would have really enjoyed the fact that their son was going to be a freshman at USC. I checked my right front pocket, to make sure my lucky key was still on board. I am going to need that in Los Angeles. I have never been there, but everything I have read or seen on the city has been cool. Coach Rolph assured me I would love the city. He told me there are a ton of things to see and do in Los Angeles. He also said the city is filled with great places to eat.

When I arrived in Los Angeles, Coach Rolph was waiting for me at the gate. He came up to me and introduced himself. He said, "Hi Dexter, I'm Coach Rolph. Welcome to Los Angeles. How many bags do you have waiting downstairs in the baggage claim?" I told him, "I only have the backpack I'm carrying." He looked at me, and for a second I saw a sense of remorse cross his face. I think he forgot I just came from the orphanage, and had very little. As we drove up the 110 Freeway headed for the campus of USC, I could see the Hollywood sign in the distance, and thought how cool was this place! The coach asked me, "Are you hungry?" I said, "I always seem to be hungry. I grew up in the orphanage where there was not much food. So, most of the time, I am hungry." Coach Rolph replied, "Well, you will never have that problem again. At USC all the athletes have their own cafeteria. That place is always stocked with food, and you can have as much as you want. I am sure you will never go hungry. Do you want to stop for some fish tacos?" I said, "Sure, I have never had fish tacos before, but really anything sounds good." We exited the freeway at Adams Street, and went left onto South Figueroa Boulevard. We stopped in a strip mall that did not look too inviting. The name of the restaurant was La Taquiza Mexican Grill. As we walked into the place you could smell the carne asada on the grill. This place smelled amazing. We ordered at the counter, then found an open table across from the salsa bar. Coach Rolph asked me, "Do you have any questions for me at this point?" I said, "I really don't, but it may be because I have just jumped off a long flight." He said, "I understand. Please know that I recognize you've had a difficult childhood. When we spoke awhile back I told you I'd be here for you. I meant that. You can call me anytime. I would like to be there for you. I would like to show you what it's like to be able to count on another person. I am not going away, and you can trust me. I am way more interested in you as a person, than just a player. I want to make you successful in life and sports. I want you to have a family again here at USC. So, please understand that I am always available to meet and talk with you." I looked at him, and really did not know what to say. I was completely overwhelmed by his kindness. I eventually muttered, "Thank you." Our food arrived and looked and tasted even better than it had smelled. I now love fish tacos and carne asada nachos!

The coach took me to my new living quarters. It was a dormitory called Webb Tower. The place looked like an old concrete high-rise building. It seemed a little out of place on the campus, because most of the buildings were brick and looked much nicer. Coach Rolph told me, this is a place where many of the incoming freshman will live. My coach told me some of the new guys on the team will be my new roommates. The campus of USC is so beautiful. It seems like a small city. Most of the kids get around on either a bicycle or a skateboard. Since I have less money than most of the homeless people that live in the area, I will walk. I was super excited about having an unlimited amount of food at my disposal. The athletes have access to this great cafeteria located right by my dorm room. I had decided to go over to the cafeteria and eat again. I think I just like the thought of being able to eat as much as I want. When I was there I ran into some of the athletes from some of the other sports, as well as some of my new teammates. Like most college students, my new teammates complained that the food was not very good. I would imagine it is because they did not grow up in an orphanage, in Lower Manhattan. I thought the food was amazing, and felt really blessed to be here.

My room had a great view of the campus. I looked down on the Lyon Center. This was a place that housed the school gym, for all the kids not competing in sports at USC. This place allowed them to work out in a great gym, that had all the right exercise equipment. As I looked beyond the Lyon Center, I could see the Uytengsu Aquatics Center. This was home to the greatest coach in USC history: Jovan Vavic. This guy was a walking legend. He coached men's and women's water polo. He has collected more National Championships then any other coach in school history. At one point, his men's team had won the National Championship six years in a row. Looking past the pools, I could see Dedeaux Field. This was the USC baseball stadium. I would find myself spending several hours each day on that field. I would attend the normal practice sessions, then roll into the batting cages and hit balls until my hands bled. I had developed large calluses on my hands, but spending hours hitting would also bring on crazy blisters and bleeding. I found myself getting lost in baseball. It really allowed me to mask my loneliness and depression. It was difficult to not think of my mom and dad. I know they would have loved watching me play baseball at USC. My dad would also have enjoyed going to the football and basketball games with me on campus as well.

I really started to notice how my teammates made the extra effort to reach out to me. They were always inviting me to hang out with them. My roommates were the same way. It was a natural connection since we spent a huge part of our day together. My teammates and I would start each day early in the morning. We met for breakfast, then went off to class. Most of our classes were done by noon. Then it was back to the cafeteria for lunch, then to practice. After practice we would eat together again, then head back to the dorms to study. The dorms and studying never really worked out. It was generally very loud, so I found myself retreating to the study rooms at the McKay Center. This center was just for the athletes. The center was named after legendary football coach, John McKay. Inside you would find all the necessary items that would make a student-athlete successful. The center housed a large study hall stocked with the latest computers and printers. It also had the athletic training facilities, along with a top-notch gym equipped with the latest weights and cardio equipment. The center was also home to all the student-athlete counselors, psychologists, weight and conditioning coaches, and the football locker room. The McKay Center was an athletes dream.

I think I'm still a little too aloof. I wasn't doing much with my teammates. I know they weren't the problem, I was the problem. I needed to be more open and trusting with people. These guys were part of my new family, and I needed to work a lot harder at developing relationships. I really never wanted to go and do much with them. Instead, I chose to spend hours in the McKay Center, lifting weights and getting stronger. I would wear myself out doing sprints on the track. I was so focused on getting drafted in the first round, and receiving a huge payday.

I am pretty sure Coach Rolph was beginning to take notice of my absence. I think he knew I was not doing much with my teammates. He called me over after practice, and invited me to his house for dinner. He said he and his wife wanted to get to know me better. I said I would be there.

I borrowed a car from my roommate, and drove to the Rolphs' home. It took me about forty-five minutes to get there. Their home was located in the town of Manhattan Beach. This is a beautiful beach city, located on the Pacific Ocean. The homes are gorgeous, and it looks like the perfect place to live. I finally arrived at their house. People complain that the traffic in New York is bad. They are correct. However, the traffic in Los Angeles makes New York look like the minor leagues. Their house was located on a street with about ten other homes. They all looked like they were custom homes, and worth a lot of money. The Rolphs' house was overlooking the beach, and the Manhattan Beach Pier. It was a great home. From the outside it was three stories tall, and had a four car garage. The home looked like something out of a fancy magazine. It was beautiful.

I knocked on the door, and Mrs. Rolph answered. She said, "Hi Dexter, my name is Anne. It's nice to finally meet you. I am glad you could come to dinner. Please come in." As I entered the house, it was as beautiful inside as it was from the outside. It looked like some kind of designer had done all the furniture, paint, and flooring, and seemed ready for Architectural Digest. This was a wonderful place to live. Anne looked at me and said, "Let me go and let Dave know you're here. Please walk around, and make yourself at home. There are a lot of memories on our walls, and we like showing them off to our friends." As I walked around the living room, there were pictures of all the National Championship victories. Pictures of the mob scenes after each game. Pictures of Coach Rolph with his players. As I walked around the living room, I secretly wished that one day soon, my picture would be on the wall with another championship celebration. The coach soon appeared. He walked down a large staircase that led into the living room. He said, "Hi Dexter, welcome to our home. I hope you're hungry, because Anne made a ton of food." I said, "I'm always hungry, and can't wait to eat." He replied, "Well, follow me, and we'll sit down. Anne said dinner has been ready for a few minutes." The coach walked me out onto a large deck that overlooked the Pacific Ocean. You could see the Manhattan Beach Pier from the deck as well. The sun was beginning to set over the water. The sky was lighting up with purple, pink, yellow, and blue swirls. It looked spectacular! This was a great night. Coach Rolph looked at me and said, "Dexter, please sit down." Mrs. Rolph had made a great dinner, and we had an amazing view to go with the meal. Mrs. Rolph asked me to tell her about my upbringing. So, I told her about my parents. Then about our home life, and my mom and dad's jobs. Then I told her about the auto accident, and growing up in the orphanage. She asked me several questions about the orphanage. Then I told her about my friend, William Biddle. Coach Rolph asked me, "Dexter, you still seem to be struggling with your loneliness. I see your teammates leaving to do things after practice, and I don't see you with them. I know they like you. I see them at practice and around the locker room. They look up to you, and appreciate all you have been through. Why are you still struggling?" I replied, "I am not totally sure. Part of me understands that I need to reach out more. Another part of me, at times, just feels helpless and worthless. I feel guilty as well. I just continue to struggle with the loss of my family. I know that I have accomplished great things. However, that really has not brought me the happiness I've been wanting." Coach Rolph replied, "Please understand that part of the curse of being lonely, is feeling worthless and helpless. You are neither worthless nor helpless. That is just what can creep into our minds when we experience loneliness and depression. I am here to tell you, that you have tremendous value. Please understand that you have been made in the image of God, and the Lord does not make mistakes. I know at times the voices in our head can tell us differently. However, when those voices are the loudest, we need to remind ourselves about the truth found in the Bible. That truth is simple. God sees you as valuable, and he loves you very much. Do you believe in God?" I said, "Yes, I do." I then went on to tell the coach how I was raised in the church, and went to Sunday school as a kid. I also told him about my lucky key. He wanted to see it, so I pulled it out of my right front pocket and handed it to him. He then went on to explain, "Dexter, you are looked upon as a leader. Your teammates believe in you. The coaches believe in you. I believe in you. You need to believe in yourself. This team has become your new family. You need to embrace that reality. I am here for you. I can never replace your father, but I will do whatever it takes to make you feel loved and welcome. You have so many great characteristics that define leaders. You are honest and humble. You are not into exaggerating your experiences. You are also hesitant to speak about your accomplishments. Those are two great qualities of a leader. You also have a positive attitude each day at practice. That shows your confidence in your abilities. A positive attitude and confidence are also trademarks of a good leader. Your teammates respect you. Embrace that respect, and rise up and lead them. If we are going to win a National Championship, then you are going to need to step up and lead. Does that make sense?" I told him, "Yes it does. I will begin to do my part. On the field and off the field. I will work on my skills as a leader." He said he was grateful for that, and believed that it would also help with my own issues. The meal ended, and I thanked the Rolphs. As I drove back to campus I could not help but compare my dad to Coach Rolph. They were so similar in nature, and both had a way of explaining things in such simple terms. I could tell my coach and his wife were special. They made me feel special. It was a great dinner. They are super people. I really like them both. Such wisdom and love.

The college years are interesting. They seem to challenge everything you believe. They also have the ability to stretch you beyond your personal safety zone. You get challenged  academically, socially, morally, and individually. It is an amazing time in life. You really find yourself having to answer the phone in the bullpen, and bring your best fastball to the mound. The game is on the line, and it is time to stand up, and deliver. Life comes at you quickly in college. You tend to grow up in a hurry. You find yourself having to make adult decisions. I am so glad I chose to attend college.

# CHAPTER
## 10

It's really hard to believe how my time at USC has flown by. It just seemed like yesterday, I was boarding a flight from JFK to LAX. Yet, the orphanage and New York seem like a distant memory. I am not sure where the time has gone. I have studied and trained a lot over the past couple of years. I have even stayed on campus for the summer. I needed to take more classes to keep up with my academic load. It's really difficult participating in athletics, at an NCAA Division I school. You have to spend a considerable amount of time training for your sport. You are also trying to maintain a strong GPA, at an academically challenging university. However, I have taken great pride in the fact, that for the past two years, I have been an Academic All American.

It is now my junior year of college at USC. Coach Rolph has assembled the best college baseball team in the country.

He spent a considerable amount of time in the off-season talking with players about our program. He had to fill several key positions on our team. He picked up a great second baseman by the name of Scott Magers. This guy can turn the quickest double play I have ever seen. He's like a Hoover vacuum at second. Absolutely nothing gets by him. He is also the most fit baseball player I have ever seen. We are so solid up the middle. I was playing the best shortstop of my life, and we looked great. We also have the top closer in college baseball. Coach Rolph signed Albert Rosario. This kid is from Puerto Rico. He stands about five feet six inches tall, and throws a consistent fastball, around 106 MPH. His earned run average is below one. This guy just rears back and throws gas. He will be a first round draft pick this June. It does not matter who Rosario faces in the eighth and ninth innings, they are not getting a run. We also had several great players returning. In left field we had a guy by the name of Dave Kingman. He was six feet six inches tall, and could hit a fastball into the next county. Dave is a huge bat in our line-up. In centerfield, we had a kid by the name of Fred Lynn. I have never seen a better outfielder in my life. This kid could also hit the cover off the ball. At first base we had a kid by the name of Mark McGuire. This guy is a monster. He hits some of the longest home runs I have ever seen. Our top starting pitcher is six feet ten inches tall. His name is Randy Johnson. He is left-handed and can absolutely dominate a baseball game.

We had a great season. We finished the season with a record of 57-3. It was the best season USC has ever had in baseball. Then we had to start playing in the postseason playoffs. In college baseball they have the Regionals, and the Super Regionals. Since our record was so good, and we were ranked number one in the country, we had the home field advantage all the way through both regionals. We beat Texas in the final game of the Super Regionals to advance to the College World Series. I wound up having a great year. All the hard work I had put into training had paid off this season. I had what many professional baseball scouts considered a perfect season. I went on to hit .470, with 37 homers, and 95 RBI. I did not commit an error at shortstop all season. Coach Rolph was notified by the NCAA that I was named College Baseball Player of the Year. I was excited about that. However, I only celebrated for about one hour. I needed to get my team ready for the College World Series. I had told myself this season would be considered a failure, unless we bring back a National Championship to USC. That means we have about one week to get ready, before we fly out to Omaha, Nebraska.

We all ate breakfast together as a team. I then gave a brief speech about staying focused when we arrive in Omaha. I also told my teammates this will only be a successful season if we return with the hardware. Nothing else will matter. I reminded them that second place is simply the first loser. We then walked to the charter bus that was waiting outside the cafeteria to take us to LAX. We boarded our flight to Omaha and landed in the late afternoon. After checking into the hotel, it was time to head to the field for practice. We had a great practice, and you could tell we were focused and ready. We made it easily through the winner's bracket, and it was on to the finals. Our opponent was going to be the Tigers, from LSU. They were a great team, that had a career season like we did. They were going to give us all we could handle.

On the way back from the field, Coach Rolph asked me to sit with him. He always sat at the front of the charter bus. He looked at me and said, "Dexter, I am so proud of you. You have done a great job this year. On the field, as well as in the classroom. I know your mom and dad would be so proud of you. You have really stepped up and become our leader. You have come so far as a player, and a person. I know it has been difficult for you. I know you still miss your mom and dad. I also know you still struggle with loneliness. I have so appreciated getting to know you. I just could not be more grateful you came to USC." I replied, "Coach, it has been my honor to play here. You have shown me nothing but kindness. You have become a father to me. Yes, I still miss my mom and dad. Yes, I still struggle with loneliness and depression. However, you have taught me so many wonderful things about life. I have been blessed to know you." Coach Rolph said, "Dexter, thank you. You mean the world to me. We have one more game to win. I need you to have the game of your life. I need you to lead your teammates to victory. I know you are ready. Let's make history together, and bring back the hardware." I said, "I could not be more focused." The coach asked, "Do you have your lucky key?" I said, "Right here, as I pulled it out of my pocket." There was no way I was going to Omaha without my key.

It was Saturday morning, and we were gathered around the breakfast table. The hotel had set up a private buffet for us. Nobody was talking. Very little food was being eaten. This was game day. We were getting ready to compete in the finals of the College World Series. I have never seen a group of guys more focused in my life. It was a great sign. This was a huge day.

The bus pulled up to 1202 Bert Murphy Avenue. This was home to the College World Series. Johnny Rosenblatt Stadium. This ballpark was legendary. This was home to the most exciting game in all of sports. So many great baseball players have been here. So many amazing games have taken place on this field. As we walked up to the main gate, the USC band was going full throttle! The students and fans had created a tunnel for us to walk through. It was awesome. They were so excited for the game. Rosenblatt Stadium looked great. The stadium seated a little over 23,000 fans. The dimensions of the park were pretty big compared to most fields. Down the left field line it was 335 feet. To center field it was 408 feet. To right field it was 335 feet. To the power alleys it was 375 feet. The fence in the outfield was twelve feet high. This was not supposed to be a hitter's park.

After the National Anthem, we headed to our dugout. It was determined that we would be the home team. This was based on our record in the winner's bracket. Each team that went to the College World Series was allowed one loss. It really was a small tournament. At the finals, you had one team that won the winner's bracket, with no losses, and one team who won the loser's bracket, with one loss. So, we occupied the third base dugout. That meant we had to play defense first. We met outside the dugout, and Coach Rolph gave us some words of encouragement to pump us up. Then we ran to our defensive positions. Our starting pitcher was Randy Johnson. We called him, "The Big Unit." This guy was nails all year long. His record this year was 19-0. He was perfect. The first batter struck out on a 95 MPH fastball. Randy had this fastball that moved so quickly in on a right-handed hitter. It was very difficult to hit. The next hitter flied out to left field. There were two outs. The final out was recorded when a weak ground ball was hit to me. We now had a chance to swing the bats. LSU sent a kid to the mound that was about six feet seven inches tall. This kid looked like he weighed about two-hundred and fifty pounds. He was a big farm kid from Iowa. He was hitting the mid-nineties with his fastball. Our leadoff man was Scott Magers. On the first pitch, he lined a ball into center field. Our next hitter sacrificed him to second. We had a runner on second with one out. I came up to bat. I told myself to just look for an inside fastball. I got my pitch and lined it into left field, and the runner scored. We were up 1-0. The next hitter was Mark McGwire. He hit a ball so hard at the shortstop, I thought it might kill the kid. He put out his glove and somehow caught the ball on one hop, and had the presence to turn a double play. So at the end of the first inning, it was 1-0.

In the top of the second inning, they managed to get a guy on with a bunt. He stole second, and came in on a single to center field. The game was tied 1-1. The next three hitters went quietly. We were now coming to bat. Dave Kingman started the inning off with a double to left center field. The next hitter grounded to short. Then Fred Lynn stepped into the batter's box. Fred was a powerful left-handed hitter. He hit a fastball about as far as any human being I have ever seen. It sailed over the right field stands, across the parking lot, and onto the domed observatory, at the Henry Doorly Zoo. It had to be about 600 feet away! The game was now 3-1. Our fans were going crazy. The second inning ended with the score, 3-1.

It was now the top of the third inning. In college baseball, the game is nine innings long. Randy Johnson was finding his groove. He struck out the first two hitters. Then the next batter doubled to right-center field. The next guy up hit a weak line drive over our third baseman's head. The runner scored. The next guy up flew out to Fred in center. The game was now 3-2. We were coming up. The bottom of our lineup went quietly, in order. The score after three innings was 3-2, we were leading.

In the top of the fourth inning, they started the inning off with an infield single. The next guy laid down a great sacrifice bunt. So, the runner advanced to second. The next batter struck out looking. The next guy hit a line drive over the left field wall. The final out was a ground ball back to our pitcher. The score was now 4-3. LSU had just taken the lead. We started off the bottom of the fourth swinging the bats. Scott Magers hit a double into the gap in right center. Our next hitter grounded to short. I came to bat and hit a line drive to right field to score the runner. Mark McGwire followed with a blast to deep center field. This thing was an absolute moon shot. He hit that ball about 500 feet over the center field wall. The score was now 5-4, the good guys. The next guy flied to right. Then Dave Kingman hit a monster home run to left field, off a hanging slider. The next batter struck out. After four innings, the score was 6-4. We were back in the lead.

The top of the fifth inning went pretty smoothly for Randy Johnson. The first batter flew out to deep center field. The next batter grounded out to first base. The last batter tried to lay down a bunt, and was thrown out. We headed to the bottom of the fifth inning. The score was 6-4. We were still leading. The bottom of our lineup went quietly. LSU had changed pitchers. In the College World Series Final, the coach always has a short leash on the pitchers. Our first batter struck out looking. The next hitter flew out to right field. The last hitter grounded out to shortstop. At the end of five, it was still 6-4.

To start the sixth inning, the first batter singled up the middle. The next hitter tried to sacrifice bunt, but popped out to the pitcher. The next batter hit a ball into the gap in right center field. The runner on first scored. The hitter went to third base, when the play went to the plate. The score was 6-5. The next batter hit a ground ball to me, and the runner from third was moving on contact. I threw him out at home. The batter was on first base with two outs. The contact play with a runner on third base is always a crap shoot. The runner is told to run on contact. The idea is that it puts extra pressure on the defense. I have seen it work, but most of the time it does not work at the college level. The next batter hit a deep ball to center field, and Fred Lynn went over the wall to bring it back. Fred had his waist up to the top of the wall and reached over to rob this guy of a home run. Keep in mind the wall is twelve feet high. The crowd went nuts. It was our turn to hit. We had the top of the lineup, coming to hit. Scott Magers was so focused at the plate today. I could not wait to see him hit. The pitcher threw him a curveball on the first pitch, and he drove it down the left field line for a double. They intentionally walked our next batter. They wanted to set up the double play. In the on deck circle, I check my back pocket. My lucky key from Mr. Biddle was still there. I hit the first pitch I saw, into left field for a single. The runner on second scored. The runner on first made it to second. The score was now 7-5. We had runners on second and first, with no outs. The next hitter hit into a double play. We had a runner at third with two outs. Our next hitter hit a deep fly to the right fielder for the final out. At the end of the sixth, it was 7-5.

Coach Rolph sent Randy Johnson back to the mound, to start the seventh inning. I could tell he was getting tired.

A huge game like this really drains you both physically and emotionally. The first batter singled into right field. The next hitter was intentionally walked to set up the double play. The next batter hit a rocket up the middle. Scott Magers dove, and was fully extended when he gloved the ball, he got to his knees, and threw a perfect strike to me covering second, and I flipped it to first for a double play. His catch was amazing. The crowd was stunned, then went wild. How he got that ball is a mystery. We had two outs, and they had a runner on third base. The next batter hit a line drive to center to score the run. The score was now 7-6. Randy was tired, but he was battling. The final out of the inning was recorded when the hitter grounded out to third base. It was now our turn to hit. It was the bottom of the seventh inning, and the score was 7-6. We were holding on. Our first batter went down on strikes, for the first out of the inning. Our next hitter got aboard on a slow grounder to shortstop. Our next hitter flied to left field. The next batter grounded back to the pitcher for the final out of the seventh inning. The score was still 7-6.

It was the top of the eighth inning. Everyone was on pins and needles. It's hard to explain just how nervous you can become as the game is drawing to the end. Coach Rolph had decided to take out Randy. It was time to bring in our closer. He was by far the best closer in college baseball. Albert Rosario is the kid out of Puerto Rico that Coach Rolph re-cruited. This kid throws a 106 MPH fastball. He is scary. There is no way you want to face this guy. He is accurate, and he is a little crazy. He will talk to himself out on the mound.

It just adds to the hitter's anxiety. This guy is a man among boys. The first batter stepped into the box, and Rosario threw him a fastball that was ten feet over his head. This pitch went halfway up the backstop, behind home plate. I thought the hitter was going to wet himself. I quickly looked at the score-board in right field, and it had recorded the speed of the pitch at 110 MPH. Good luck trying to hit that! Rosario threw the next three pitches down the middle, for a called third strike. He was throwing so hard, the sound of the catcher's glove was echoing throughout the stadium. The next two batters went down swinging. They were not even close to hitting the ball. This kid was throwing gas. It was our turn to hit. The bottom of our lineup was due to hit. The first batter hit a ball off the left field wall for a long single. The next hitter sacrifice bunted him to second. The next batter hit a weak grounder to second. The runner advanced to third. Our num-ber nine hitter fouled off a couple pitches, before he dodged a wild fastball. The pitch got past the catcher, and the runner from third scored. The batter eventually was thrown out on a ground ball to shortstop. The score was now 8-6. We had our insurance run for the ninth inning.

We had reached the top of the ninth inning. The crowd was on their feet cheering. Both the USC fans, and the LSU fans. The Tigers were sending up the top of their lineup to face Rosario. This was their last chance. Albert was in full-crazy-mode. I could hear him from shortstop getting pumped up. He was screaming at himself. He was behind the mound, looking out towards center field, yelling. The more crazy he got, the more our fans went nuts. You have to love baseball! The first batter swung at the first two fastballs and missed. He then hit a groundball to the first baseman. One out. The next hitter fanned on three straight fastballs down the middle. Two outs. I looked at the scoreboard, and Albert was throwing a ridiculous 108 MPH. Our catcher had the entire offseason to ice his hand. The final batter stepped to the plate, and our fans were going bananas. The crowd noise was so loud, I could no longer hear Albert screaming at himself. The first pitch was a called strike. The second pitch was fouled off down the first base side. The final pitch was clocked at 112 MPH, and taken for a called strike three!

The USC Trojans were National Champions! We had just won the College World Series! The celebration began. We all met at the pitcher's mound for the party. Guys were jumping on each other, and hugs and high-fives were everywhere. Our fans poured onto the field. They wanted to join us in the celebration. This was such a great feeling. It's a feeling you never want to end.

Once the field was cleared, we all lined up to shake the hands of the LSU players. They had played well, and we wanted to make sure we showed them the respect they'd earned. We then had to line up for the trophy ceremony. The NCAA had asked Harold Reynolds to present the trophies. Harold was part of the broadcast team. He had also been a great baseball player. He was known as the "Mayor of Omaha". The first trophy he presented was for the Most Valuable Player. This went to Scott Magers. He had an absolute monster of a game. He'd played the best defense I had ever seen. His play up the middle saved the game for us. He also punished the pitchers in all of his at bats. Scott was the perfect pick for MVP. The next trophy presented was for the whole team. It was the National Championship trophy. We all went forward to receive the trophy. Then we lined out for the photographers to take our pictures. All the parents came onto the field, to have their pictures taken with their son and the trophy. It was a happy time for everyone. I really wished my mom and dad could have been here to see this take place. They would have been so proud of me. It would have been fun to take our picture together with the trophy. Coach Rolph asked me to come over and take a picture with him and his wife. He would later send me that photo in a nice frame. It quickly became one of my prized possessions. I always had it hanging next to the picture the pediatric nurse had taken of my mom, dad, and sister Rebecca.

I believe the greatest lesson I have learned in college is simple. A person's family can come in many different forms. Sometimes it can be a single mom who is working three jobs and just barely making it. Other times it can be an orphanage full of boys. It can be a baseball team. A family can also be a sixteen-year-old girl who made a mistake one night, and wants to do the right thing. It can also be a loving coach and his wife, wanting to make a difference in the life of a player. Families are good. They make a difference. Families change lives. The family is a tremendous gift. Families are a blessing.

# CHAPTER
## 11

It was time to leave Omaha, and head back to Los Angeles. There was a big celebration being planned in our honor. USC loves to celebrate their champions, and we were no exception. When our plane landed in Los Angeles we had a bus waiting to take us back to the campus. There was a large group of students, faculty, and alumni waiting for us in front of Heritage Hall. This was the place on campus that housed all the great USC trophies. Our trophy was going to take its rightful spot, next to the enormous bronze statute of Tommy Trojan, that occupies the main lobby. When we arrived on campus we could hear the band playing as we drove up to the hall. The crowd was cheering, and this was a true hero's welcome. The ceremony would start by having the president of the university speak. Following the president would be various city officials, then Coach Rolph. We had brought the

National Championship trophy with us from Omaha, and it would be placed into Heritage Hall. The school would also place my College Player of The Year trophy in the hall as well. It was a tremendous honor to be part of the Trojan Family.

As the ceremony ended, a lot of the guys had asked me to join them at different celebration parties. I chose to decline and just hang back at Heritage Hall. All the people were gone, and it was just me sitting on the steps in front of the building. So many thoughts had been running through my mind. I had so wished my mom and dad could have seen me honored today. They would have been proud of me. I really miss them. As I sat on the steps outside Heritage Hall, I pulled out my lucky key. I held it in my hands and just stared at it for what seemed like hours. I had really thought that going to USC would change my life. I thought winning the College World Series and Player of the Year would bring me joy. I was wrong. I was still lonely. I was still sad. I was still lacking hope. My location had changed, but not my outlook. It felt strange. I would never have thought I would still feel this way.

Today was the draft for Major League Baseball. Once again, this was being held in New York. They had chosen the same hotel as before. The Ritz-Carlton, Central Park. The university had set up a room for all of us to watch the draft. They had the cafeteria stock it with all sorts of great food and soft drinks. I had been contacted by several teams and knew that they were interested in signing me in the first round. I had contacted and signed with two of baseball's best agents.

They were Bob Coyle and Scott Allen. Bob was the financial genius, and Scott was the best contract negotiator in sports. These guys were the best in the industry. They represented the best players from all the major sporting leagues. Scott would negotiate the contracts, and Bob would steer the players' investments. So, Scott had been in contact with a couple teams that wanted to sign me in the first round. The office of Major League Baseball had asked me if I would come to New York, and be present during the ceremony. I had to finish up my finals, and told them I would not be able to attend. Scott had told me they were disappointed. They believed I would be one of the first players chosen in the draft. They really wanted me to be present in New York for the show on television.

The tension in the room was getting a lot more heated. The time was drawing near for the draft to start. It was also going to be a sure bet that Albert Rosario and Scott Majors would be high draft selections. Some of my teammates were trying to break the tension by cracking jokes. Although it was difficult to appreciate their jokes, It was easy to appreciate them. They were trying to distract us all from the stress of the day. This was my future. This is what I had dreamed about as a young boy. This is what I had worked at for so many years. This is what I'd told my dad I would do for a living. It was all coming down to today. The day had arrived. I looked at Coach Rolph, and he smiled and winked at me. As we looked to the big screen televisions hanging in the room, we saw the Commissioner of Major League Baseball walk to the podium. He said, "Good evening ladies and gentlemen. My name is Fay Vincent, I am the Commissioner of Major League Baseball. This is the June draft for Major League Baseball. I declare the draft to be open. The Los Angeles Dodgers are on the clock." So, the draft had started, and the Dodgers had five minutes to make a decision. There are usually forty rounds in the draft. There are thirty teams in Major League Baseball. So, the draft will last a couple of days. My agent, Scott Allen was working his cell phone in the back of the room. I could see him making and receiving dozens of phone calls. He was talking to the different teams that wanted to draft me. His job was to secure the best contract and deal he could. The Commissioner came back to the podium to announce the first pick in the draft. He said, "The Los Angeles Dodgers have traded their first round position to the New York Mets. The Mets are on the clock." The crowd in the hotel ballroom went crazy. They were hooting and yelling with excitement. They were all the Mets fans in New York, that went to see the draft in person. I could see Scott in the back of the room with the cell phone glued to his ear. He was giving me the thumbs up sign. I had no idea what that meant, but he looked happy. I saw the camera men turn the cameras on in our room. Major League Baseball had sent a camera crew to USC, to send a live feed back to New York. Commissioner Fay Vincent went back to the podium. He said, "With the first pick, in the first round, the New York Mets select from the University of Southern California, Dexter Hightower." The room went crazy! I was the very first pick in the first round, and I was going to the Mets! The Mets! My teammates piled on me like I had just scored the winning touchdown in the Super Bowl. I was going to play professional baseball for the New York Mets! The cameras were rolling, and the Mets fans in New York were going nuts as well. The kid from Queens was coming home to play ball. This was amazing! It was so much fun being surrounded by my teammates, Coach Rolph, and my agents. It was a truly great day.

The week had gone by very quickly. My agents had been contacted by several news agencies that had requested interviews. We tried to accommodate as many as we could. The agencies that were the most fun, were the New York outlets. They were as excited as I was for me to return to the Big Apple. They had also been running stories about me growing up in Queens, and all that had happened to my family. My phone was ringing and it was Bob Coyle. I picked it up and said, "Hi Bob, what's up?" He said, "The Mets are ready for you to sign your contract. Scott has negotiated a huge signing bonus for you." I asked, "What's that?" Bob said, "When you are a top draft pick, the team that drafts you will always give you a large bonus. The Mets have agreed to pay you a signing bonus of $35,000,000." The phone went silent for a moment. I replied, "Are you kidding me?" Bob said, "No, I am not kidding you. That is what we have agreed to sign the contract for." I could not believe the amount of money they were going to pay me. I thought about that and realized, I don't think I have ever had even $100 dollars in my wallet. In my life, ever! I told Bob, "Thank you, and please also thank Scott as well." I literally had no idea what I would do with that kind of money. I just wanted to play baseball for the Mets. It was a busy week, and I still needed to pack up my dorm room and get ready to head back to New York.

As I was packing up my dorm room, and getting ready to leave USC, there was a knock on my door. I had about four hours before I needed to catch my flight to New York. My agents had scheduled me to attend a press conference with the Mets. As I opened the door, I saw Mr. William Biddle standing there with a smile on his face. He gave me a big hug. Then asked, "Do you have time to talk?" I said, "I always have time to talk to you." So, I invited him into my room and offered him a chair. He said, "Congratulations on a great career at USC. Also, on being drafted by the Mets. I followed all of your games. I really enjoyed watching the College World Series." I asked, "You were there in Omaha?" He said, "No, I watched on television. It was a great game, and so much fun to see you and your teammates celebrate on the pitcher's mound." I asked, "What brings you to USC today?" He said, "I had a few people I needed to see in Los Angeles, so I decided to stop by and see you too. How have you been doing since the last time we spoke?" I replied, "I have been working on a number of positive things. I have been trying to use the gifts I have been given by God." He said, "Why don't you explain what you mean." I said, "Well, take leadership for instance. I know that I have been given that gift. I have tried to use it to help my teammates. I have tried to provide them with a good example both on and off the field. I have tried to show them the importance of being both a good student, as well as a good athlete." Mr. Biddle asked, "Are you still struggling with loneliness and depression?" I said, "Yes I still struggle with that. I really thought it would have gone away by now. I thought being successful would take away both of them. However, winning a College Baseball World Series did not. It was fun to win, but it did not change how I have been feeling. My teammates and coach have been a blessing. However, I still really miss my family. I have continued to carry that pain with me. I have also continued to carry my lucky key with me as well. I think about it every day. Some days I pull it out, and just stare at it. The key always brings a smile to my face." Mr. Biddle replied, "Dexter, I am glad you continue to carry your key. I am also glad it continues to bring a smile to your face. When you talk about your gifts, I see the excitement in your eyes, and hear it in your voice. That is what makes this life worth living. You need to continue to use your gifts to bless others. When you use your gifts to bless others, it also blesses God. He has given you those gifts to be used and exercised. When you do this, you will feel alive. Your gifts are designed to give you purpose. When you use them, you are fulfilling your purpose in life. When you fulfill your purpose in life, you are blessing and showing love towards other people. When you love others, you show your love for God. He has made you in his image. He has created you for a purpose. He has given you great gifts. He wants you to use those gifts. Love and bless others with your gifts. This will allow you to take the spotlight off yourself. Does this make sense?" I said,

"Yes it does. I am trying to do this each day. What about the pain I am experiencing?" He said, "This life will always have pain associated with it. The rain falls on the heads of the just people, and the unjust people, equally. You will never be able to control the pain and tragedy in your life. The reason for this is simple. You cannot control the presence of evil. This has been around since Adam and Eve. They decided to eat a piece of fruit from the tree of the knowledge of good and evil. Just like you were taught in Sunday school. It goes back to the book of Genesis. So, you have to trust God in all things. In the good times, as well as the difficult times. He loves you, and has given you tremendous gifts to bless others with. Does this make sense?" I replied, "Yes it does. Thank you for taking the time to explain this to me. It really means a lot to me. You have been such a great friend to me." Mr. Biddle replied, "Dexter, I am so proud of you. You have blessed me and so many others. I know your mom and dad would be proud of you too. Please come and visit me when you get back to New York and find a place to live." I said that I would. I then walked him to the door, and we gave each other a parting hug. I went back to packing. I could not help but smile each time I thought of what Mr. Biddle had taught me.

When we discover our individual gifts, this life begins to make perfect sense. We have all been given different instruments to play in God's orchestra. Some of us will play the violin, while others will play the flute. And others will play a clarinet, or a trumpet. If the only instrument that is playing is the kettle drum, it won't be much of an orchestra. We all have to be willing to exercise our gifts. When everyone starts to exercise their gifts, this allows us all to find our purpose. When we all find our purpose, the orchestra begins to play beautiful music. Beautiful music changes hearts. Beautiful music changes lives. Beautiful music can change the world.

# CHAPTER 12

The New York Mets had made the decision that I was not going to spend any time in their minor league system. What that meant for me, was I had just been told that when the season started, I would be on the big league roster. Apparently this decision was made by the executives, and was announced at my press conference. The press conference went well, and they made sure I was properly prepped for dealing with the media. I have to say for someone who has stayed away from the limelight, it was a little uncomfortable staring into all the cameras. However, there was huge excitement in the city over making me the first pick in the draft. There were lots of stories in the newspapers and on television. It's not that common that a local kid grows up and plays for his favorite team. So, it was definitely exciting for me. It was also exciting for the city. The city was alive and buzzing.

I had not been back to New York since I'd left the orphanage, and headed to Los Angeles to attend USC. So, coming back was exciting and odd all rolled into one. When I'd left New York as a kid, I was looking for a fresh start. I was looking for purpose in my life. I was running away from loneliness and depression. Now, I was returning a multimillionaire. A guy that was going to be playing professional baseball for his beloved Mets. No doubt a lot of things had changed in those years I was gone.

I think one of the most odd things about returning home, is I expected to see my parents. That sounds weird. However, for most of my early life they had always been here. So, coming back and not seeing them was difficult. The world was coming at me fast and furiously. After I signed the multimillion-dollar contract, everyone wanted a piece of my time. All sorts of individuals and groups, wanting me to come here and there, for photo shoots and speeches. There was also the crowd that wanted me to give them money. Everywhere I traveled, women would randomly approach me wanting a date. So, it has been a little stressful. I am adjusting to my new life. I am learning to deal with the different situations. I am also learning that I will never be able to please everyone.

The last time I saw my mom and dad was the night they were killed. We had just been out to dinner, and were driving home. That is when the crash took place. I never saw them again. I was taken by ambulance to the hospital. I was then placed into a medically induced coma, because of the bleeding that was taking place in my body. Then a decision was made to have their funeral without me, because no one knew how long I would be in the coma. The doctors also informed the people making the decisions on behalf of my parents, that the trauma from the accident, mixed with the trauma of my parents' funeral, would be too much for me to handle. So, they moved forward with the funeral, and I was not able to attend. So, the last time I spoke to my mom and dad was that night at dinner. The last time I saw them was the same night. It just seemed a little too strange to wake up out of the coma, and be told everything you used to have was gone. No mom, no dad, no home, no school, no friends, no Queens, and by the way you will now be living at the orphanage in Lower Manhattan. Crazy! It was all just really overwhelming. I don't think there is any way to prepare yourself. I don't think anyone could have done anything different. It was just a really difficult situation. There is no script for what took place. I think everyone was trying to be as sensitive as possible. Sometimes in life, you just have to deal with some really bad things.

I had just two things on my personal agenda since returning to New York. My agents had about a thousand things for me to do, but I had just two. The first thing was to visit my mom and dad's grave. The second was to purchase a condo to call home. The Mets have been very gracious to me. They have been housing me at the Waldorf Astoria. I have a beautiful suite there, and it is a first class property. The problem is, I will also need a tax break, with all the money I am now making. So, I will need a place of my own. I will need to write off the mortgage interest. I will also need a very expensive place. I am not comfortable with a really expensive place. It is simply not who I am. However, Bob and Scott tell me it is absolutely necessary. So, I will push forward on a new place to live.

I decided today was the day I was going to visit my mom and dad's graves. I had blocked off the entire day to make this happen, and told myself that I didn't need to rush. It's funny how rushed you become when life speeds up. I pulled up to Christ our Redeemer Cemetery, on Laurel Hill Boulevard in Queens. At the front of the property was a giant iron gate, with a cross on top. The cemetery was on four-hundred and fifty acres, and overlooked the entire city of New York. The sign said it was consecrated by the Archbishop in 1845. Whoever made the decision to bury my mom and dad at this place, knocked it out of the park! This cemetery was beautiful. I stopped at the gate, and asked directions to the location where my parents were laid to rest.

I drove up the hill past hundreds of grave stones, until I had reached the summit. There was nothing but green grass and grave stones, as far as my eyes could see. As I arrived at what I thought was the location, I got out of my car. I walked over a few rows searching for my mom and dad. I was blown away at what I saw next. My mom and dad were buried right next to my sister, Rebecca! I was overcome with emotion. My only response was to fall to my knees and cry. Rebecca had died in the hospital shortly after being born. She was my older sister. My mom and dad were buried on either side of her.

It was beautiful. It was so emotional seeing them all together in the cemetery. I missed them so much. I wished we could all be together. What a great surprise to see them all together again, as a family.

It was time to drive home. I had stayed at the cemetery for the entire day, and spent most of the day talking to my parents. In a different way, it was really comforting. I can't remember ever taking the time to talk to them, since they had passed away. The situation allowed me to speak to them in an open and honest way. I was able to share with them the different things that had been happening in my life. I filled them in on my time at the orphanage. I told them about what it was like to have to leave our old neighborhood in Queens. Leave my school, and friends. I told them about my high school, and about playing baseball. I told my mom about dating Kelly. I told her she would have liked Kelly. I went on for a long period of time, telling them about winning the State Championship in baseball. I had also mentioned how the Dodgers had drafted me out of high school. I told them about attending USC, and how Coach Rolph had really taken me under his wing. I told them about the many times he and Mrs. Rolph had me over for dinner. I told them about how special the Rolphs made me feel. They made me feel like I was their son. I told my dad how cool it was to attend USC, and win the College World Series. Then I saved the best for last. I replayed the entire draft day for my mom and dad. I told them about signing a contract with the Mets. As I was telling them all about this, it felt wonderful. I had never said these things out loud before. It made me feel like they were listening, and this really mattered to them. I could sense their love and approval. I felt proud to be able to give them such a great update. I also went on to tell them about my lucky key. I told them about how Mr. Biddle had continued to be a source of love and kindness in my life. How he continued to visit me, and encourage me. It was a really great day. It was fun getting to see their graves, and such a blessing to see Rebecca. I left there with a smile on my face. I felt really blessed to have such a great family.

I woke up this morning, realizing it was time to do one of the first grown up things in my life. I had to buy a home. Nothing really prepares you for this type of transaction. The largest place I had ever lived in was the home I grew up in. The home was about nine-hundred square feet. Then it was the orphanage, then my dorm room at USC. This was where my agent came to the rescue. Bob Coyle helped me find the perfect place. I wanted to live in the city. I felt like old people with kids moved to the suburbs. I wanted to be a short cab ride away from the stadium. I also wanted to be close to all the great restaurants and coffee houses. I wanted to feel the pulse of the city. What all that meant was pretty simple. I would need to find a condominium. The condo would have to be in a nice area, and cost a small fortune. Bob had recommended a new condo, that was located on the Upper East Side of Manhattan. I decided to meet him there to take a look. As I arrived to the location on East 74th Street, it was a picture of success. This place had state-of-the-art security, and a lobby that rivaled the finest hotels in the world. The lobby was home to a coffee shop, a dry cleaner, a gym, a bakery, and a small market. They had really thought of everything. After being greeted by the doorman, I took a private elevator to the 65th floor. That was the location of the 7000 square foot condominium. This joint was crazy beautiful. The views from this place were amazing. From the windows in the living room, you looked down on Central Park. You could also see across the Hudson River, into New Jersey. Bob began to show me around the place. This condo had five bedrooms, and seven bathrooms. The place had professional designers take care of absolutely every detail. They had brought in special furniture, fixtures, and works of art. The designers did not miss a thing. This place could be in any magazine. Bob told me it came furnished, with all the art work as well. That was appealing to me, since I had nothing. I also had zero desire to go shopping for any of this stuff. All the beds had linens, and the bathrooms all had towels. The kitchen was designed for a gourmet chef, and was fully stocked with dishes, pans, pots, and silverware. This place was truly ready for someone to move in and not miss a beat. This place was fancy! Bob told me that I could afford this place. So, I wrote a very large check that day. I was a property owner. I left feeling very grownup!

Coming back home always conjures up visions of grandeur. The idea of arriving at a place you're familiar with and have great memories of. It seems so warm. So inviting. So comfortable. Sometimes you realize that home is not what it used to be. It's at that moment, you realize home was all about the people, not the location. Sure, the memories took place in a certain geographical location. However, the great memories were a result of the loving people that surrounded you, when they were made. The magical feeling of coming back home, is the result of the loving people that await you when you walk through the front door.

# CHAPTER
## 13

I was now in my third year with the Mets and things were going well. I had adjusted to life in the Major Leagues. I know that seems like an odd statement. How difficult could it be to collect millions of dollars and play baseball? I guess it's like anything in life, it simply takes time to adjust. My typical day is not very typical. During the season I play 162 games. Half of those games are at home in New York, and the other half are played in cities around the country. The games are generally played at night with a 7:05 P.M. start time. I have to be at the ballpark about three hours before the game. During that time I will start by eating dinner. When I am playing at home or when I am on the road, I can eat in the clubhouse. In both cases, we are provided a chef that will cook our meals. The really odd thing is when we are on the road, our team secretary provides each player with about three-hundred dollars a day for meals. Yep, as much money as we make, the team still provides us with meal money. I suppose it's no different than the business executive who pulls out his company credit card to purchase meals. It's just a perk of being a professional. I tend to eat the food in the clubhouse. I also had to get used to sleeping in different hotels and beds. This took some getting used to as well. Don't get me wrong, it's a great life. It is just different than what I had been used to. It's also great not having to study for classes any longer. I have a ton more free time on my hands. When I am done eating I get ready for practice. I will start out stretching, then begin to run. This allows my body to get warmed up, and ready to play. At that time, a coach will begin to hit me ground balls at shortstop. This helps me get my arm warmed up and ready to throw as well. It also allows me to get used to taking ground balls on the various fields we play on. Each infield plays a little differently than the others. Then I move into batting practice. This affords me the opportunity to see some pitches and practice spinning the bat. When I am done, I head back to the clubhouse to shower, and put on my game uniform. My routine never really changes. This helps me stay consistent, and prepare both physically and mentally for the upcoming game. We then gather as a team, and allow our coaches to give any final words of wisdom. This usually involves instruction about the pitcher we are going to see that night. We are told what the strengths and weaknesses of the pitcher have been in the past. We are also told what type of pitch to look for in certain situations. There is quite a bit of preparation that goes into getting ready for a game. The average fan might think we just put on our uniform and line up for the National Anthem, then play the game. It's a little bit more complicated than that.

We had a great season this year and were heading for the World Series. The entire city was alive and excited about baseball. We'd had a very good season, and our team had won over a hundred games this year. So, we were definitely ready to play. We had made it through the various playoff games without too much difficulty. As a team we were playing some solid baseball. The World Series is an amazing animal. It's hard to believe the amount of press, and television networks that cover the event. The last time I heard, the game was going to be broadcast in 228 different countries and 19 different languages. So, you can imagine the amount of reporters that have converged on New York. I have been getting requests for interviews from dozens of media outlets. It is incredibly difficult to focus on the very thing that pays my bills: baseball. All the attention comes from the fact that the fans want to know what is going on inside their favorite ball clubs. Baseball is such a worldwide sport. There are so many countries represented on each team. It's also the only hope for many kids making it out of their particular situation in life. Baseball has been a true blessing to everyone that has reached this level of play. It has provided a lifestyle that does not even exist in many of the countries that are represented. As a result, the fans of baseball are always interested in the lives of the players. Baseball provides a tremendous escape for the average fan. It's also why fantasy baseball has been such a big thing. This allows the average fan to play manager and stay involved in the game. Again, a great way to escape the boredom of daily life.

As a player I have always strived to take care of my body. I will only eat certain things, and have not allowed myself some of the daily foods most people consume on a regular basis. I also take certain vitamins and supplement to keep me strong and full of energy. As a result you really get to know your body, and what makes you run at such a high level of competition. When your body isn't feeling the way it should, it sticks out like a sore thumb. I'd noticed for the past couple of months that I hadn't been feeling particularly well. I realized that when I would run during my workouts, I would fatigue much quicker than normal. I also was having pain in my stomach. A couple of weeks ago I got on the scale to weigh myself, and had lost about eight pounds. I really attributed it to the stress of a hundred and sixty-two game season, along with the looming World Series. I had also not been eating very healthfully since the media appearances had demanded so much of my time. The end result was, I could tell something was not right with me. I really did not want to see one of our team doctors. I have the best medical care at my fingertips, but refused to go see the doctor. I knew there would be dozens of tests they would put me through, and I didn't want to find out what was wrong. That would only lead to me missing games, and being a distraction to my team. In baseball you tend to beat your body up quite a bit over the long season. You will always have one injury or another. Since it is a little bit of a macho game, you just learn to suck it up and play ball. You understand as a player that the other guys are doing the same thing. It is so difficult to get to this level of baseball, that you don't want to give the team any reason to take you out of the lineup. The last thing you want to happen is to wind up on the disabled list. So, I have been trained to play on, and ignore the pain and discomfort.

The week before the World Series was to begin in New York, I received a call from my college coach. I hadn't spoken to Coach Rolph since I'd last seen him at USC. He told me we were long overdue for a talk, and asked if he could come over and meet with me. He said he had flown to New York to try and recruit a couple of players for the upcoming season. I told him it would be great to see him again. We had agreed to meet the following day at my house. The doorbell rang at about 8:00 A.M. the next morning, and when I answered the door it was Coach Rolph. He looked like his dapper self and walked in and gave me a warm embrace. I offered him some cappuccino, and we both sat down in the living room to catch up on what has been going on in my life. Coach Rolph started the conversation by saying, "Dexter, this is a beautiful home. I'm so happy you found the perfect place to settle down. How have you been doing now that you're back home in New York"? I said, "I have been doing well, and trying to settle into the big league life." It has not been easy, but I think I am getting used to the different cities, and the pressure." He said, "How are you feeling physically? Is your body and mind ready for a World Series"? I replied, "I think it is. Although I have been having problems with fatigue, and I can tell something is not right with my body. I have been losing weight." He said, "I know you probably have not seen the team doctor. However, please make sure you see him after the season is over." This is what I loved about Coach Rolph. He understands the pressure a player is under to perform at this level. I said, "I fully intend on seeing the doctor when this is all over." He then asked, "How have you been doing with your loneliness, and the loss of your mom and dad? I know you had to be confronted with that when you returned to New York." I said, "Yes, I was definitely confronted with that. I went to see where they'd been laid to rest. I also saw that my sister was buried between my mom and dad." He replied, "That's great, I bet you never thought you would have seen that." I said, "No, I hadn't anticipated that, but it was a pleasant surprise. I had a great conversation with my parents that day. It has really helped me heal. I am not completely healed, but it sure helped." He went on to say, "Please understand that you'll never fully be healed from their loss. However, I can tell you they'd be very proud of you and all you have accomplished. I'm proud of you too. You've really had to overcome so much to get to where you are today. You've done an amazing job! Be proud of yourself and your accomplishments. Very few people in this life have been through what you've been through, and have been able to attain the success you've attained." I said, "Thank you. You've been such a blessing in my life. You've allowed me to feel human again. I never thought that was going to be possible. I appreciate all you've done to mentor me. It's difficult to put into words what your love has meant to me. I consider you to be a second father to me. Thank you." He replied, "Dexter, I consider you to be my son. I know we've gone long stretches without getting a chance to talk, but you're always on my mind. I've spent a great deal of time praying for you. I know you're going to play great in the upcoming series. You're a special man, and a very special baseball player. Use your adversity in this life as a motivator. Allow yourself the margin to feel lonely, but then use that feeling to rise above." I replied, "Thank you. I'll do my best. Since you're in New York, please do me the honor of staying here with me. I'll get you tickets to every game, and you can travel with my team to the away games as well." He said, "It would be my pleasure." I said, "Great! Let me show you to your room. I'll have my concierge go and get your luggage from the hotel." Coach Rolph said, "That would be great."

The World Series was now in full swing, and we were locked up with the Boston Red Sox. The series was tied three games to three, in a best of a seven game series. The final and deciding game seven was headed back to New York and Shea Stadium. If I thought the hype was out of control before the series started, it was absolutely crazy now. The Boston Red Sox had been a big favorite to win the series, and it was now tied up and coming back to our yard for all the marbles.

I had been having a good World Series for my team, but my health was getting worse. I still didn't want to tell the team doctors. My biggest fear was they would tell my manager, and

I'd be on the bench for game seven. My health would have been a huge distraction for my team. The pain had gotten worse in my stomach, and now I had blood in my stools. It seemed like I was constantly fighting fatigue. However, I had managed to be hitting at a torrid .420 clip for the series, and that was with 10 RBI. My team was on fire, and we wanted to be World Champions. We could taste it, and did not need any unnecessary distractions. This was the World Series, and I would suck it up, then get some help in the off-season. I continued to repeat the catch phrase that had been coined by Tug McGraw. He was one of our pitchers. He had come up with the phrase, "You gotta believe." I continued to repeat that phrase over and over in my head. I would pull out my lucky key, look at it, and say, "You gotta believe."

It was a beautiful night for game seven. I drove onto Roosevelt Avenue and saw the lights of Shea Stadium glowing from my car. I got goosebumps running down my arms, and a lump in my throat. At that moment, all I could think about was attending all those Mets games with my dad. He would have been out of his mind to be with me in the locker room, as I was getting ready to try and help my team win another World Series. It was at that moment, I pulled off the road. I began to cry, and just stared at the stadium in wonder. I knew in my heart, that my mom and dad were watching me today. I told myself that this day, and my performance in game seven, was dedicated to them. I told myself this was going to be a great night, and I would be driving home to-night a World Champion. I repeated the phrase, "You gotta believe." Then I pulled back onto the highway, and headed for the stadium.

After batting practice, I was called over to do a pregame interview with Vin Scully and Joe Garagiola. They were doing the television broadcast for the game. I had a hard time focusing on their questions, because I could not believe they wanted to talk to me. These men were the legends of baseball, and I got to be interviewed by them before the game! I was in awe. What an amazing experience. These two men were a huge part of what has made baseball so much fun to watch. They were great!

It was now time for the National Anthem. The color guard had brought out a huge American flag. It covered most of the outfield. They had also brought out a grand piano and placed it in center field. Ray Charles was announced as the person who was going to sing the anthem. When he walked out, the crowd gave him a huge applause. Both teams had been announced and were out of their respective dugouts for the anthem. My teammates and I occupied the third base line, and the first base line was occupied by the Red Sox. When the anthem was finished, a fly over took place. It was the United States Air Force. They were flying four of their finest jets over the stadium. It was amazing to watch. We then headed for the dugout to begin the game.

Since we were the home team, we started on defense. Our starting pitcher was a guy named Doug Irwin. He was a great pitcher. His record this year was 24-2. The Mets had picked him up in the middle rounds of the draft. He was a bargain. He had pitched for a small college in San Diego, by the name of Point Loma Nazarene University. Since it was a small school, Doug had not received the attention he deserved. The Mets knew he was good, and got him relatively cheap. He was a gamer. He threw a fastball in the mid-nineties, and had a curveball that went from twelve o'clock to six o'clock. When this pitch was working, he was very difficult to hit. The Red Sox' first batter grounded weakly to me for the first out. The next two hitters were called out on third strikes. It was the perfect beginning to the game. It was now our chance to hit. The first batter up in our lineup, singled to center field. He then stole second on the first pitch. Our number two hitter grounded out to second. The runner advanced to third base. I was the third guy up in the inning. I hit a curve ball into the gap in left center. The run scored and I was standing on second base. The next two hitters up, both struck out. At the end of the first inning it was 1-0, we were ahead.

To start the second inning, the middle of the Red Sox' order was coming to bat. The first guy up hit a line drive down the third base line for a double. The next guy up struck out. Doug was throwing hard. The next batter hit a fly ball to deep right field. The runner on second advanced to third base. There were two outs. The next batter hit a blooper over the head of the second baseman to score the run. The next batter hit a ground ball back to Irwin, for the third out. The game was tied 1-1. It was now our turn to hit. We had the middle of our lineup coming up to hit. Our first batter hit a ground ball to short for the first out. The next hitter struck out. The third batter up hit a fly ball to left field for the third out. The game was tied 1-1.

Starting off the third inning, the Red Sox had the bottom of the order coming to bat. Irwin struck out the first batter on the fastballs. The velocity on his fastball had picked up to about 97 MPH. The next hitter grounded out to me at short for the second out. The pitcher was now at bat. He struck out on four pitches. It was now our turn to hit. We also had the bottom of our lineup coming to bat. Our first hitter hit a foul ball that was caught by the third baseman for the first out. The next hitter grounded to short for the second out. Our pitcher was now up. He hit a line drive to center field for the final out of the third inning. It had become apparent that this was going to be a pitchers' duel.

The Red Sox were back to the top of their lineup. The first batter hit a single to right field. The next batter bunted him to second for the first out. The next hitter, hit a line drive down the third base line, that was caught by our third baseman, who threw back to second from his knees, for a double play! It was a great play. It was our turn to hit. Our first batter grounded out to shortstop for the first out. The second hitter reached first base on a walk. I came to bat. The third base coach had given me the hit-and-run signal. The runner from first left on the pitch, and I hit a line drive into center field. The runner on first made it to third. We now had runners on first and third base. The next hitter hit a towering fly ball to center field that scored the runner from third base, and I advanced to second. The next batter struck out. After four complete innings, the score was 2-1, we were leading.

To start the fifth inning, the Red Sox were at the heart of their batting order. The first batter up hit a line drive into center field. The next batter followed with a single to right field. I called time out, and went to settle Irwin down. It seemed to work. The next guy up hit a ground ball to our third baseman who tagged his bag and threw to first for a double play. The Red Sox now had a runner at second with two outs. The next batter hit a weak fly to right field for the third out. The score remained in our favor, 2-1. The middle of our lineup was coming to bat. Our manager was a man by the name of Carrol Land. He was a baseball genius. He gathered the hitters together before the inning, and told them to be patient. He stressed that they needed to allow the game to come to them. Our leadoff guy hit a line drive to left field for a single. The next batter up laid down a perfect sacrifice bunt, advancing the runner to second. The next hitter struck out. The next guy waited on a high curve ball and hit it into the left field stands. Both runs scored, and are fans went crazy! The Red Sox went right to the bullpen and brought in relief. The score was now 4-1. When you are a manager in game seven of the World Series, you have a very quick hook. The next batter struck out, to end the inning. After five complete innings, the score was 4-1. We had the lead.

To start the sixth inning, the Red Sox were sending the bottom of the order up to bat. Doug Irwin was in prime form. The fist hitter grounded out to second for the first out. The next hitter struck out on a wicked curveball. The next guy flied to deep right field for the final out. It was our turn to hit. We had the bottom of the lineup coming up. Our first batter grounded out to first. The second hitter lined to short for the second out. The next hitter was Irwin. The pitcher threw him a fastball down the middle, and the next thing you saw was the ball landing in the left field seats. Doug was as shocked as anyone. He stood at home plate until the ball hit the seats. Coach Land yelled at him to run. It was really funny. The next hitter struck out. The score was now 5-1. We had a comfortable lead going into the seventh inning.

Irwin took the mound to start the seventh inning. The Red Sox had the top of their lineup coming up. The first batter singled to center field. The next batter up hit a line drive past our third baseman into left field. They now had runners on first and second. The next guy struck out. The following hitter lifted a fly ball to deep center field for the second out. You could tell Irwin was getting his fastball up in the strike zone. That is a sure sign a pitcher is getting tired. Our pitching coach made a visit to the mound. Our pitching coach was a man by the name of Mike Chapman. He had forgotten more about pitching than most guys knew. He called for a meeting of the infield on the mound. He was delaying the game on purpose, so we could get guys up in our bullpen. The next batter up hit a monster home run over the center field wall. The game was now 5-4. Everyone in the ballpark knew Doug was done. He'd pitched a great game, and had simply run out of gas. Coach Land came to the mound and signaled the bullpen for a pitcher. Doug walked off the mound to a standing ovation. Our fans were so knowledgeable. They knew he'd thrown a heck of a game. Our relief pitcher was named Marty Brown. This kid joined us halfway through the season. We had traded a couple of great prospects to the San Diego Padres to get him. He was nails. This kid threw strikes, and got outs. We needed him to get to our closer. Marty got the next hitter to strike out looking on three of the most nasty sliders I have ever seen. At the end of the top of the seventh, the score was 5-4. We still had the lead. The seventh inning stretch was now in progress. The Mets had Christian recording artist, Anson Sexton, sing "Take me out to the ballgame." His music is loved throughout the world. Our fans loved it! We then sent the heart of our batting order to the plate. Our first guy up hit a double down the third base line. It was now my turn to hit. As I reached into my back pocket, I could feel my lucky key. I continued to tell myself what Coach Land had been saying, "Be patient, let the game come to you." The pitcher threw me a 2-0 curveball, and I hit it about 500 feet over the center field wall. The score was now 7-4. The best feeling in the world is circling the bases after you hit it out. The next guy up hit a ground ball to short for the second out. The next batter struck out. At the completion of the seventh inning, the score was now 7-4. We had some insurance runs.

At the top of the eighth inning, the Red Sox were sending the middle of their lineup to bat. Marty Brown was as focused as I have ever seen him. He got the first hitter to ground out to the first baseman. The next guy up hit a weak line drive to me for the second out. The next hitter up took a curveball that did not break over the right field wall. The score was now 7-5. The next guy up hit a line drive to the left fielder who made a diving catch. The crowd went nuts! We now had the bottom half of our lineup coming up. The first guy struck out on four pitches. The next guy hit a ground ball to third for the second out. Coach Land then sent in a pinch hitter for Marty Brown. That guy wound up flying to right field for the final out. The eighth inning was now in the books. The score was 7-5. We had the lead heading into the ninth inning.

At the top of the ninth inning, you could feel the excitement in the air. The fans could smell blood in the water. There was not a single person sitting down in the entire stadium. Our closer was running full speed from the bullpen, and that just pumped up the crowd even more. It was so loud in the stadium it was hard to think. Our closer was my old teammate from USC, Albert Rosario. He had signed after USC with the Mets. They had a second pick in the first round that they used to sign Albert. This guy was a stud. He had collected forty-nine saves this year. He'd set a new Major League record. Albert was going nuts on the mound. He had faced the center field wall and was just screaming. I had no idea what he was saying, because it was simply too loud. It was classic Rosario. He was one part Hollywood, and two parts crazy. The fans loved him! The first batter did not have a chance. He struck out looking on a 107 MPH fastball. The

Puerto Rican was throwing gas. The next guy up swung at a 108 MPH fastball, and it sawed his bat in half for a weak ground out to Albert. There were now two outs. Albert was screaming again, and the crown noise was deafening. The next hitter took the first fastball for a called strike. The scoreboard read 111 MPH. The next pitch was fouled off down the right field line. The count was now 0-2. The final pitch was a fastball recorded at a whopping 115 MPH, for a called strike three! The crowd went nuts! We rushed the mound, and the celebration began. Fireworks were going off as we celebrated the victory with a large dog pile on the mound. The Amazing Mets were World Series Champions!

The team from my childhood were champions again. It was an amazing feeling as we went back to the locker room for the crazy champagne-spraying celebration and party. Before I left the field, I asked security to go and get Coach Rolph from his seat. We embraced each other with a hug, then walked arm in arm into the tunnel for the celebration. I was a World Series Champion. Everything had come full circle, right back here in Queens. Right back to the place where I grew up loving baseball. My beloved Mets were back. Simply amazing! Words cannot explain the joy I felt that night. Everything I had worked so hard to obtain, had come to fruition. I was on top of the world.

There is no substitute for hard work. When we are determined to work hard, we will accomplish our dreams. Hard work is always at the center of any successful person or venture. Without hard work, we are relegating ourselves to mediocrity. Hard work produces greatness. The enemy of greatness is always mediocrity. Greatness is achieved when we get it into our heads that nothing will stand in our way. Champions are never born. They are created out of hard work. Hard working people will never settle for mediocrity. They understand that greatness is the only goal. May hard work, honesty, integrity, and character, always be our standard.

# CHAPTER
## 14

The month following the World Series has been a whirl-wind. The parade New York City threw for us was amazing. It was such a fun day for the players. The fans also enjoyed themselves. Millions of Mets fans lined the parade route, and everyone had such a great time. It's hard to explain what it is like when you see the parade route. All the players and their families are in cars going down the parade route. The fans are not only lining the streets, but they are also dropping confetti from the buildings. They are hanging out windows, on light posts, and rooftops. It really made for a fun experi-ence. The parade ended at Shea Stadium. The stadium was packed when we all drove into the stadium. The mayor gave a speech, and all the players and coaches were announced. It was one of those days everyone came together to celebrate all the great things baseball represents. It was a great day to be a baseball fan.

After the World Series had ended, the Mets made it very clear that they wanted to renegotiate my contract, and wanted to do it right away. They'd told Scott Allen they wanted to lock me into a long-term contract. Since I was enjoying New York, and things were going well, I was very interested. I told Scott I didn't want to play for anyone but the Mets. Scott advised me to take the deal. He said the money was going to be astronomical. So, I went ahead and signed the deal. When the contract was signed and done, the Mets were going to guarantee me $250 million dollars over the next seven years. The Mets had decided I was the future of their franchise. They wanted me to be around for several years. Everyone seemed happy with the new contract but me. I of course loved the actual contract. However, I was getting sicker by the day, and still did not have the time to deal with my health. Since the announcement of this huge contract, everyone just seemed to take up my time each day. I found it very difficult to carve out the time to go see the doctors. When I received this new contract, it really opened the doors to lots of endorsement deals. So, as a result, my days were full of meeting with the companies that wanted to give me millions of dollars to represent their products. Also, I think part of me didn't want to go see the doctors. I knew the news wouldn't be good. I had based my opinion on the fact that blood kept showing up in my toilet bowl. I was getting sicker. I continued to lose weight. I was so tired. It took everything in me to get out of bed in the morning. I was really not interested in facing reality. I was enjoying the attention, and I was also enjoying the large contracts. This is what I had been working so hard to achieve. Now it was happening, but it was impossible to enjoy. I knew I needed to get checked out. I needed to face my fears. I needed to start feeling better.

I finally had the courage and conviction to go see the doctor. I blocked the time off in my schedule. The night before, I had invited Scott Allen and Bob Coyle over for dinner. I told them everything I'd been going through with my health. When I was done talking, they were shocked. They both told me that tomorrow we were going to see the doctor. They agreed to pick me up in the morning, and sit in on the appointment with me. I was relieved that I'd finally told them. I was also happy they wanted to come with me. I could tell they sensed the stress in my voice, as I shared my health problems. They are not only great agents, but true friends. I was lucky to have them by my side.

I got up this morning, and felt worse than ever before. I barely had the energy to take a shower and get dressed. As I was dressing, I made sure to take my lucky key. When the guys arrived to pick me up, they told me we were going to see Dr. Justin Butorac. He's the top doctor in all of sports. Patients travel to his medical clinic from all over the world, seeking treatment. He served as Chief of Staff at the Mayo Clinic, in Rochester Minnesota for years. He then left for New York to start his own clinic. He is also the official doctor of the Mets. So, I knew I was in very capable hands. When we arrived at his facility, I felt so much better. I was finally facing my health issues. I felt relieved. I told Dr. Butorac about what had being going on with me for the past several months. I told him about the stomach pain, fatigue, and the constant blood in my stools. He immediately sprang into action. He called a special meeting with his staff, to give them a briefing on what was taking place with me. The staff began testing me that day. It was very comprehensive, and lasted most of the day. I was wiped out at the end of the day. Dr. Butorac advised me to go home and rest. He also asked me to come back tomorrow for more testing, and a possible diagnosis. Scott and Bob drove me home, and we agreed to meet at my place in the morning for round two.

I went home that night, and thought about everything that had taken place in my life up to this point in time. I thought about my great childhood, my perfect mom and dad, and my perfect life before the car accident. I also thought about my time at the orphanage, and going to USC. Winning a College World Series. I also thought about the day I was drafted by the Mets. I remember how much fun that day was for me. Then winning the World Series. Then being rewarded by the Mets with a $250 million dollar contract. On the outside, everything seemed to be perfect. Like the great ending to a perfect dream. I had become so successful. I had the type of money and fame most people could only dream about. I could buy anything I wanted. I could travel anywhere in the world by private jet. I could stay at the finest resorts in the world. I could eat at the best restaurants. I could afford any car, jewelry, or clothing I desired. However, on the inside I was a different person. After all the success I still was not very happy. I was still wondering if this was all life had to offer. I could not shake the thoughts of why I was not happy. Why I was not on cloud nine like my teammates. Why was I still so lonely? Why did I miss my family so much? Why could I not be happy like other people? Eventually, I fell asleep on my sofa watching television.

In the morning, Scott and Bob had to wake me up. I needed help showering and getting dressed. We then left the house and headed back to the medical clinic. When I arrived at the clinic, Dr. Butorac greeted me. Then the testing resumed. At the end of the testing, Dr. Butorac asked me to join him in the conference room. Scott, Bob, and the doctors on staff arrived to discuss the results. The main doctor who began the discussion was the oncologist. He was the top oncologist in the city and widely considered the best in the world. Dr. Butorac had spared no expense when he assembled his team. As he began to speak, he discussed the tests I had taken and the results of those tests. He told me in the kindest, most gentle way possible, that he was one hundred percent certain I had colon cancer. When he was done telling me about my diagnosis, the room went silent. Everyone was looking at me. I had no idea what to say. My head was spinning. I was thinking, colon cancer was for older people, not me. I am a pro baseball player, we don't get cancer. As my head was going through a million scenarios, I was literally dizzy. The awkward silence must have been too long.

The oncologist began to speak again. He went on to tell me that my cancer was aggressive, and in the final stages. He said they would recommend a very aggressive chemotherapy treatment as well as surgery. I just sat there numb and unable to speak. I looked at Bob and Scott, and they looked like they had just seen a ghost. This was horrible news, and there was no way to spin this any other way. This was bad. I was dying. Dr. Butorac went on to explain how sorry they were to give me this news. The room was silent again. I could not speak a word. I could not even get a question out of my mouth. This was really happening. I was in deep trouble. I was dying. Bob and Scott were eventually able to get me out of my chair, and to the car. They brought me back home and put me to bed. They both insisted on spending the night at my place. I was too shocked to disagree. The last thing I remember was my head hitting the pillow.

I did not know it at the time, but Scott had called Coach Rolph that night to tell him my diagnosis. Coach Rolph had told him he'd be on the next flight out of Los Angeles. He was determined to be at my side during this crisis. Scott told my coach they'd arrange for a private jet to pick him up at LAX.

Bob came to my room the next day to wake me up. He said that Coach Rolph was here to see me. I asked if he could help me take a quick shower and get dressed. When I walked into the living room, Coach Rolph embraced me with a big hug, and tears in his eyes. He said, "Dexter, I am so sorry. The moment I heard, I sat down and cried with Anne. Please know that I will never leave your side. I am here for you. I love you." With tears in my eyes, I managed to say, "Thank you." Coach Rolph somehow gained his composure, and we sat down on the sofa. He said, "Dexter, as bad as this diagnosis is, you cannot control the results. Cancer does not have the ability to rob you of your character. Cancer will never be able to shatter your hope. It will never destroy your friendships. Cancer will not be able to take away the love you have for your family. Cancer has no power over your good memories. Cancer cannot steal your courage and peace. Cancer has no power over your soul, and no way will it ever destroy your faith in God. This diagnosis has been a shock to all of us, but it did not catch God by surprise. He is still here, and he loves you more than ever. Now is not the time to give up. This is the bottom of the ninth inning, and the bases are loaded. You must fight with everything in you, to drive in the winning run. You are a champion, and now you must fight this like the champion you are. You have just been knocked down with an inside fastball at your head. It is time to get up, brush the dirt off your uniform, get back in the batter's box, and swing for the fence. You are a Trojan, and Trojans Fight On." I looked at my coach, and said, "I will Fight On!"

After several weeks of chemotherapy, and constant pain, the decision was made to go forward with surgery. When I was awakened after surgery, it was clear to me I was still in dire straits. My body was killing me, and the nurse informed me that they had just given me a large dose of morphine. She told me the doctor would be by later in the afternoon to check on me, and answer any questions. Dr. Butorac arrived just before the nurse was to drop off my dinner. The thought of eating was so foreign to me. I was simply not hungry, and the pain was overwhelming. The doctor said to me, "When they opened you up on the operating table, we were shocked at how much cancer was in your body, and how aggressively it had spread. We made the decision that any further action was going to be in vain, and might even lead to you bleeding to death. There were just too many tumors. We could not believe how quickly the cancer had spread throughout your body. We made the decision to close you back up, without removing any of the cancer." As he was telling me this, I could hear him saying it, but it didn't seem real. Bob and Scott were beside me the whole time, asking questions quicker than trial attorneys. The bottom line came when Dr. Butorac said, "Unfortunately, we've done all we can do for you. I hate to give you this news. However, I wouldn't be doing my job correctly to withhold this information. I believe it is now time for you to get your affairs in order. Please use whatever time you have left to say goodbye to the people you love. I'm not sure exactly how much time you have to live. I do know it is not very long. You'll be able to go home in a couple of days. I've also reserved a bed for you at Mercy General Hospital, in Lower Manhattan, right off of William Street. Again, Dexter, I am so sorry to have to give you this bad news."

I had nothing to say. I looked at Bob and Scott, and asked them to go grab the car so I could go home. I wanted a few days at home, before it got so bad I would need to get to the hospital. I knew once I checked into the hospital, I would never be going home again. I realized the doctors wanted me to stay a few days in the clinic, to recover from the surgery, but that was not an option. I needed to make the most of the time I had left to live.

After arriving home, I asked Scott to call my attorney, Steve Goodman. I asked him to have Steve come over tonight, to deal with my affairs. I then went into my bedroom and collapsed on my bed, and cried. I couldn't believe my health had deteriorated so rapidly. I was really going to die. My life was coming to an end. It was now time to deal with this reality. I needed to get my estate in order. This was really the end. It is hard to explain my feelings. This came so quickly. I am still in shock. However, I cannot ignore the reality of the situation. I must face this like a champion. I would have never guessed my life would end like this.

Steve Goodman was kind enough to clear his busy schedule, and arrived later that afternoon. We went to work on the final paperwork for my trust, power of attorney for healthcare, and finances. I asked Bob Coyle to be my power of attorney as well as the executor of my trust. I made sure Steve drew up a DNR for my healthcare documents. I did not want to place Bob in any difficult situations that may arise. I hurt so badly now, that the thought of my life being prolonged by machines gave me a headache. We needed to take several breaks since I was in such terrible pain. Steve and my agents were troopers. I had instructed my attorney to leave twenty percent of my estate to the New York City Police Department's Widows and Disabled Officers Fund.

I told him to donate this money in the name of Sargent Robert Hightower. Then I instructed him to donate another twenty percent to the Queens Unified School District. This donation came with the stipulation that the money be used to fund playground equipment and class supplies for all the schools in the district. I asked that the money be donated in the name of Norma Hightower. Then I told him to donate another twenty percent to the Children's Hospital of New York. I asked that this money be donated in the name of Rebecca Hightower. The final forty percent of my estate was to be donated to the Holy Sisters of the Faith Orphanage as well as every other orphanage in New York City, divided equally between them all. I then asked Steve to give my condo and ten million dollars to Coach Rolph. Steve had his secretary, paralegal, and notary present. So, the final documents were completed and signed. I thanked them as Scott and Bob walked them to the door. My body was now in so much pain I could hardly make it to my bedroom. I told Scott we needed to get to Mercy Hospital in the morning. When I got to my room, I just laid in my bed. I felt awful. My body was killing me. I heard a knock at the door. It was Coach Rolph. He asked, "Dexter, can I come in?" I said, "Yes, please come in." He walked in and sat next to me on my bed. He said, "I'm so sorry to hear about the news you received today. I know you're in pain. I know your entire body feels terrible. Please understand this one thing. I could not be more proud of you." He then reached over to my dresser, and grabbed my lucky key. He said, "put this in your pocket" I said, "thank you." He replied, "You have been through so much adversity in your life. You have dealt with that adversity better than anyone could have imagined. Your life has been a struggle. Your life has been difficult. You've dealt with heartache and pain, the likes of which most people will never know. Yet you've remained positive, and always tried to make the most of your situation. You worked your tail off, and became one of the best baseball players to ever live. You've been a great example to me, and everyone who has ever known you. It's been my pleasure to call you my friend. In a world filled with turmoil and darkness, you've been a shining light for good. You have fought the good fight. You have run the race of your life. You have finished well. You will always be a champion to me. I'll never forget you. Son, I love you." In tears, I managed to say, "Thank you for always being there for me. I love you too." We then embraced in a hug. Coach Rolph sat there holding my hand, until I had drifted off to sleep.

I know it sounds trite and cliché to say, "Life is short." However, it is. So many times we refuse to do certain things that seem too time consuming. We don't want to waste time. However, when those "things" involve people we love, we need to reconsider. Our jobs have a way of controlling our schedule. They can at times, be overly demanding. They give us the perfect excuse not to go and enjoy our son's Little League game. They make for the perfect excuse not to attend our daughter's recital. We have the ability to talk ourselves out of birthday parties, anniversaries, church, and weddings. All in the name of our precious schedules. Time has a way of always marching on. It will continue with or without us present. Let's never arrive at the end of our lives with a list of regrets. Make the effort to be kind. Be loving. Be courteous. Walk humbly. Show mercy. Let's take the time to watch a beautiful sunset. Let's take the time to go on a hike. Let's take the time to tell those close to us, how much we love them. Life is short, so let's remember to number our days. Let's really work at making every day count. Life is a gift.

# CHAPTER
## 15

I didn't realize it at the time, but my friends could not wake me up in the morning. When they finally got me out of bed, I could not walk. I could not talk. Coach Rolph had to dress me. Scott went and got the car. Bob somehow secured a wheelchair, and managed to get me down to the car. I was in bad shape. They delivered me to the hospital that day, and the room that was reserved for me by Dr. Butorac was ready.

I had a difficult few days in the hospital. It may be the most difficult place on earth to actually get sleep. The machines and alarms never stopped going off in my room. I am not even sure why they continued to go off. I just know it was really difficult to get any sleep. The noise of other patients that were in pain, never seemed to end. My pain was in full bloom. I felt miserable, and my breathing became more labored. It was impossible to talk, and getting even more difficult to breathe. Coach Rolph sat on the side of my bed very patiently, just holding my hand. He understood I could not talk, but sat there so I would not be alone. As difficult as my situation was, he was a calming and loving influence in that hospital.

I heard the alarms going off again. The beeping was at an all-time high. The machines I was hooked up to were going crazy. My room became a flurry of activity. I could hear the nurses in a full blown panic. One nurse yelled out that she could not find my pulse. I heard a doctor screaming for oxygen. I heard so many voices in the room. I felt secure, because I could still feel Coach Rolph's hand squeezing mine. Then the room went silent. I could no longer hear the machines beeping. I could no longer hear the nurses panicking. The doctors' voices went mute. The other patients' voices were gone. There was nothing but silence in the room.

Friends are a gift from God. They observe us at our best, and sometimes at our worst. Friends are there for us in all of life's challenges. Friends stay with us through thick and thin. Friends have the ability to cheer us on to great personal victories. Friends are also there to lift us up during difficult times. Friends bring perspective to our lives when things don't make sense. Friends love us at all times. Friends tend to know our strengths and weaknesses. Friends are great at speaking into our lives. Friends show us compassion and grace. Friends understand the power of words. Sometimes, friends don't even have to speak a word to show their love. Friends make our lives worth living. Friends add value to all of our experiences.

Friends are amazing. Let's remember to love and appreciate them. You will never understand the value of friends until you need them most. Friends are to be cherished. They are our greatest asset. Friends are a blessing.

# CHAPTER
# 16

When the doors swung open at the train station, I was looking at a stone-paved path. The path was winding through a grove of olive trees. It was so peaceful just walking along the stones. The trees were filled with different birds that were singing. They didn't seem bothered as I stopped along the way to observe them. I didn't recognize what type of birds they were, but they were very colorful. They just sat in the trees and sang. They ranged in color from bright yellow, to ocean blue. They were beautiful. The path continued to wind through the olive trees. As I continued to walk, I could hear running water. It sounded like a stream or river. It was just a gentle running of water. As I heard the water, I began to get thirsty. When I came around a corner I saw the stream. It was winding through the olive trees. I stopped beside the stream to bend down and taste the water. It was so clear and perfect. I cupped my hands together to draw the water from the stream. As I brought the water to my mouth, I could tell it was cold. The temperature of the perfect glass of water on a hot day. I drank the water. It was the best water I have ever tasted. As I was drinking the water, I noticed something moving in front of me. I stopped and looked up to see some deer. They had stopped by the water's edge to drink. They were young fawns. Their color was a beautiful light brown. They noticed me, but I did not seem to bother them. They just continued to drink. It was such a different experience. I had lived my entire life in the city, and you simply don't see wildlife in Manhattan. I was blown away by their beauty. They seemed so at peace with their surroundings. After watching them for some time, I decided to keep moving forward along the path. The path continued to wind through the olive trees. The trees were a magnificent green color. The leaves were moving from the slight breeze that was blowing through them. The path was now completely in shade from the trees. The shade with the slight breeze, made for a really pleasant experience. It seemed to be the perfect temperature. As I came around another turn in the path, I noticed something ahead. It looked like a really large gate. There was an unusual glow coming from the gate. It was still about a couple hundred yards away. However, the closer I got, the glow became brighter and brighter. I could tell the glow was a bright golden color. The path seemed to be ending at the gate. The olive trees seemed to continue to line the path all the way to the gate. I arrived at the gate when the path ended. The gate was enormous. It looked about a hundred feet tall. The width of the gate was about a hundred yards long. Then all you could see for miles in either direction was a solid gold wall. I now understood why I could see the gate from so far away. The gate was solid gold! I had never seen anything like it before. It was so incredible! The gold was beautiful. It was polished to perfection. I had to touch it. As I reached out to touch it, my hand just glided along the smooth surface. As I looked up at the base of the gate, it was next to impossible to see the top. Looking up, I saw stones that were embedded in the gate. They started about twenty feet up the gate. It was all sorts of precious gems. I saw sapphires, rubies, emeralds, chalcedony, sardonyx, beryl, topaz, and millions of large diamonds. It was spectacular to look at, and it was so shiny. The stones just seemed to enhance the glow. This gate must have cost millions of dollars to build. As I took a few steps to my right, I noticed a sign on the gate. The sign was about three feet high and six feet wide. I did not notice it before, because the sign was solid gold. Just like the gate. The sign had writing on it. The writing was in block letters. The letters were all done in precious stones. The sign said, "Welcome to the Emerald Garden. In the Emerald Garden, there is no more death, nor sorrow, nor crying. There is also no more pain, for the former things have passed away." The sign was as beautiful as the words written on it.

I studied the gate for what seemed like hours. It was incredibly difficult to take your eyes off its beauty. There was simply nothing to compare it to. I tried opening the gate by pulling really hard. The gate would not open. Then I noticed that the gate had a lock. I was wondering how I would get into the Emerald Garden. It was at that time that I heard a noise come up from behind me. I looked behind me, and standing there was Mr. William Biddle. I could not believe my eyes! In that brief moment, I thought I was dreaming. Then he spoke to me. He said, "Dexter, it's so good to see you again. I've been waiting for you. Did you enjoy your walk along the path?" I said, "It's good to see you again as well. What a pleasant surprise. Yes, I really enjoyed my walk along the path. I also enjoyed the water from the stream." He then said, "Dexter, you have fought the good fight, you have finished the race, and you have kept the faith. I am so proud of the person you have become. You've endured so much pain and loneliness. You've been a blessing to so many people. Please check the right front pocket of your jeans." I then reached into my pocket. As I pulled my hand from my pocket, I was holding my lucky key. The gift he had given me. The key I had taken everywhere with me. To baseball games, practices, dinners, and to the hospital. I took my lucky key, and placed it into the lock. I turned it to the right, and the golden gate slowly opened. Mr. Biddle looked at me and said, "Dexter, welcome to your new home. Welcome to the Emerald Garden."

The golden gate swung open. I was standing in the most beautiful place I had ever seen. This place was amazing! I'm not sure I can even bring justice to it with my description. In the middle of the Emerald Garden, was a man who sat on a throne. His hair was white like wool, as white as snow. He had on a full-length white robe, with a golden sash.

Around his throne were twenty-four other thrones. On those thrones were twenty-four men clothed in white robes, with golden crowns on their heads. Proceeding out of the main throne was a pure river of water, clear as crystal. There was this amazing rainbow around the throne as well. The rainbow was brilliant in color. It looked like nothing I had ever seen. It's like the colors were in high definition. Then around the main throne, and the twenty-four other thrones, were tens of millions of people. There were so many I could not count them all if I tried. They were all worshiping God and singing songs. There were so many different people groups, yet they were not divided. They seemed so unified. They were one people. The languages were all different, yet everyone could understand the others' languages. It was the most incredible sound I have ever heard. Tens of millions of voices, singing songs we sang at the church I went to as a child, lifting up their voices in perfect harmony. I was blown away at how magnificent they sounded, the perfect choir, as they all stood worshiping God. Sometimes the people stood up and raised their hands, and at other times they fell on their faces in awe. When they were on their faces, I heard them saying, "Blessing and honor and glory and power be to him who sits on the throne, and to the lamb, forever and ever." Then others would shout out with joyful voices saying, "Hallelujah! Salvation and glory and honor and power belong to the Lord our God." It was so beautiful. So powerful. So utterly amazing. This place was filled with joy and peace. The people were happy, and filled with wonder.

As I continued walking through the Emerald Garden, I realized I was walking on streets paved in solid gold! The streets were pure gold, and looked like transparent glass. I noticed there was no sun or moon. The entire place was illuminated by the glory of God, who sat on the throne. Everywhere I looked there were fruit trees. Apples, oranges, bananas, figs, grapefruit, and nectarines. Also, there seemed to be a never ending supply of the nicest green and red grapes I have ever seen. These trees and vines made perfect fruit. I stopped to pick an apple. As I bit into the apple, the juice came flowing down my face. The apple was so crunchy. It was the perfect piece of fruit. The type of apple you were always looking for in the grocery store. The fruit trees and vines were being watered by a river. The river was winding through the orchards. There were so many trees, counting them was impossible. The river had the best tasting water I have ever swallowed. It must have been the same water I drank on the path that led to the gold gate. It was amazing! I continued to walk around the garden. It was so enormous. It went on for ever. As far as my eye could see. It was filled with perfectly green grass and rolling hills. I decided to continue to walk around and explore the place. I was feeling great. Just like the sign said on the gate, my pain was gone. I walked up one hill, and could not believe what I saw at the top. It was a herd of sheep that were lying down. That in itself was not amazing. What was amazing was the enormous lions that were next to the sheep! They were not attacking the sheep. They just laid there sleeping. The odd thing for me, was that I was not afraid of them. They looked at me and went right back to napping. I stood there in wonder. I literally could not believe what I was looking at. They were just hanging out together. As I started down the hill into the valley, I saw a herd of zebras running by me. They looked like they were just playing and getting some exercise. The last time I saw a zebra was at the zoo in New York. I continued to walk along the valley floor. The grass felt so cool on my bare feet. I am not sure what happened to my shoes, but I was glad they were not on my feet. The grass felt amazing. It smelled like the fresh-cut grass at Shea Stadium on Opening Day. It made me want to play a double-header. As I continued to walk, I came upon some wild horses. They were beautiful. They came right up to me as I was standing next to some trees. The trees were different fruit trees. I looked for an apple tree. I wanted to pick some apples and feed the horses. I found the apple tree and picked three apples. The horses loved them. They also loved me. They were using their long necks to nuzzle up against my body. It was so cool. I had never touched a horse before. They were so great. I decided to hike up another hill. When I got to the top, I looked down into the next valley. The valley was covered with what looked like really large homes. I wanted to get a closer look. Walking down the hill, I came upon a grove of pine trees. I heard several voices coming from the trees. I decided to investigate. Walking into the trees, I saw an opening. When I looked through the opening, it was a golf course. The course was gorgeous. It looked nicer than Augusta National Golf Club. That is where they play the

Masters each year. The fairways were so green, and you could not see one imperfection in them. The bunkers were glowing white. It looked like they had been filled with the finest, crushed white marble. There were several men, women, and young kids playing golf. Those had to have been the voices I was hearing. They were all having a great time. The course was lined with the most beautiful flowers I have ever seen. The colors were just exploding. What a place to play golf. After watching a few foursomes tee off, I decided to press onward. As I came closer to the large homes, I heard more voices. This time it was clear that the voices were coming from children playing. I came around a path, and found kids playing baseball. There were about twenty of them. They had a field that was set up, and they'd divided into two teams. The kids were really enjoying their game, and all seemed to be having the time of their lives. A couple of the boys came up to me to say hello. They looked like great kids. I decided to walk down the gold street next to their baseball field. The kids had told me it led to their houses. As I was walking down the street, it was obvious how large these homes were. They were not ordinary homes. These places were mansions. They were huge. They looked like those colonial mansions you see in the South. Each home had a perfectly manicured lawn. All the homes had white picket fences. In many of the homes there were front porches, with swings. Many of the children were out front playing on the lawns. Every property sat on vast amounts of acreage. There was plenty of room between each mansion. As I passed one home, the owner was out front, and waved to me. His dog came running up to me. It was the cutest French Bulldog you have ever seen. She was so full of life, and just wanted to lick me. This was the nicest neighborhood I had ever seen. As I passed the various properties, everyone would wave at me. The people were so friendly. It was so inviting. The Emerald Garden was a wonderful place.

I continued to walk down the street. I was astonished at what I saw next. It stopped me dead in my tracks. In the yard of the next mansion was my mom! She looked at me, and we both started to run towards each other. The whole time she was yelling for my dad. We met at the front gate of their yard. She threw her arms around me. I could not believe what was happening. My mom and I continued to hug. She could not stop kissing and hugging me. She finally said, "Dexter, it's so good to see you again. I knew you'd find us. I have waited so long for this moment. I've been praying for you." I said, "Mom, words cannot explain the joy I am feeling right now. My emotions are going crazy. I've missed you so much. A day has not passed, without me thinking of you and dad. I've spent so many lonely nights thinking about you guys." The next thing I knew, my dad was hugging me. Neither of us could talk. We just held each other tight. He finally got out the words, "Son, welcome home. We have missed you every day. Our hearts have been longing to see you. I'm so sorry to have left you behind." I said, "Dad, it wasn't your choice. I knew you'd never leave me behind on purpose. I lived every day knowing how much you and mom loved me. You guys are so special." My mom turned to me and said, "Dexter, I want you to meet your sister Rebecca. Come into your new home, and let me get her. She is just waking up from a nap." We walked into the house together. It was amazing how I felt. I was happier than I have ever been. The loneliness was gone! My life was complete again. I was home! As we entered the house, I noticed how beautiful it was inside. This was nothing like the apartment in Queens. It was also a lot nicer than my condo in Manhattan. This place was amazing. My dad and I sat in the living room waiting for my mom. She arrived with Rebecca. My mom said, "Dexter, meet your sister." I was overwhelmed with emotion. My hands were shaking as my mom handed her to me. She was so beautiful. She had these dark blue eyes, and her little bald head was black with hair. Her cheeks were red, and she just stared up at me. It was so great to finally meet her. She was a beautiful little baby girl, perfect in every way. I continued to cradle her, as I settled back into the sofa. My dad looked at me and said, "Dexter, it is so good to see you again." My mom said, "We've been dreaming about this day for so long." I said, "I can't believe we're back together again as a family." My dad said, "We've been watching you for so many years. We are so proud of what you accomplished. I know how difficult it was for you to be left behind. We saw your struggles, and continued to pray for you. Our hearts were filled with such joy, the day you decided to accept Mr. Biddle's gift. We were overwhelmed with gratefulness." I said, "That was the single most important decision of my life. Without you guys, I'm not sure I would have been able to make that decision on my own. You guys had given me such a strong foundation for life." My mom with emotion in her voice said, "Dexter, I'm so sorry you had to grow up in the orphanage. It broke my heart to see that. I was praying for you every day. I was trusting in the Lord to bring you comfort and safety. I saw how you struggled, and I know it wasn't easy." I said, "Mom, thank you for praying. Clearly, God answered your prayers. Yes it was difficult, but my memories of you and Dad made it easier. Mr. Biddle was so gracious to be there for me. His visits were always a great emotional lift." My dad said, "I'm so glad I took the time to tell you the stories about him." I replied, "Dad, it was because of your stories that I was able to accept his gift." My mom said, "Oh Dexter, we have so much to talk about. I can't believe you are finally here. Tell us about your time at USC." I said, "It was so much fun going to school there, and getting to play baseball. It truly is an amazing university. Dad, you would have loved going to my games. You would also have enjoyed watching my school play football. They are so good. The best part about attending USC, was the friendship my coach provided. He's an amazing man. He taught me how to be a leader, and a man." My dad said, "Yes, Coach Rolph is a blessing. We were so grateful the day you signed with USC. When you arrived in Los Angeles, and Coach Rolph met you at the airport, we knew our prayers had been answered. I will be forever grateful for that godly man. He stepped in and filled the role I was not able to complete. He is a true blessing from the Lord." My mom said, "Was it cool to win the College World Series?" I said, "It was so great! You would have really enjoyed going to Omaha. We had such a great team. Dad, you would've been blown away by our team." He said, "I am sure of that. Your team sounded amazing." I said, "I think the best memory I had at USC was the day the Mets drafted me. Dad, can you believe I got drafted by the Mets?" He said, "Dexter, I was so proud of you that day. It brought up so many wonderful memories for me. I loved taking you to Opening Day." My mom said, "Dexter, what was it like to walk onto the field at Shea Stadium for the first time?" I said, "It felt magical. It was like I was in a dream. I couldn't believe I was really taking ground balls at shortstop." My dad said, "Tell me what it felt like to be a World Series Champion." I said, "Dad, the feeling was unbelievable. I had never worked harder in my life. My team worked hard all year. So, to have won game seven in Shea Stadium, was a dream come true. Our fans were so great." My mom said, "What was your victory parade like? Did you enjoy it?" I replied, "Mom, you've never seen more people crammed down the streets of New York in your life. They were everywhere. The mood was fantastic! People were so happy that day. It seemed like everyone in New York came out to celebrate our victory. It was truly a great day. You would've enjoyed watching me ride down Park Avenue." My dad said, "Mr. Biddle was at the game, and said you played great. He loves baseball. I would've really liked to be there with you that day. We had so many great baseball memories. Your mom and I were so proud of you that day." After my dad said that, Rebecca began to stir. My mom said,

"It's time for her to eat. Let me go get her a bottle, and you can feed her." My mom went into the kitchen to get the bottle. When she returned, I popped the bottle into Rebecca's mouth. She looked happy. I couldn't believe I was feeding my sister. My dad said, "Dexter, please also know how badly we felt when you were told you had cancer. It really tore us apart. We prayed for you on a daily basis. We knew the Lord would work things out, but we also knew that you were in a lot of pain. We saw you suffering. We knew it was difficult for you. We also knew you were a fighter." I said, "It was horrible. However, I was surrounded by great people who cared for me. They loved me. They supported me. They did everything in their power to bring me comfort. They were a true blessing." My mom said, "Yes, they are a blessing. It made us feel so much better knowing you had that support. Those folks are great. It is so good to see you again." After she said that, she came over to hug me again. My mom said, "I have to check on dinner. I have a roast in the oven. I have been cooking all day long." I said, "Why have you been cooking all day long?" She replied, "To celebrate your homecoming. We are having a huge party tonight. I have invited all the neighbors." I said, "How did you know I would be here today?" She said, "Mr. Biddle told me." I said, "How did Mr. Biddle know?" She said, "You will have to ask him tonight. He was the first guest I invited." My dad looked at me and said, "Dexter, follow me up the stairs, I will show you your new bedroom."

# CHAPTER
# 17

The hospital room was completely silent. The nurses were no longer yelling. The doctors were worn out. The machines that had been beeping and spitting out numbers, had gone silent. The entire hospital team had done their very best. Today was one of those bad days on the job. The type of day where you can be on top of your game, but it still is not enough. The type of day you grow to really dislike. Everyone in the room was looking at the floor in utter exhaustion. Their heads were hanging low. They had seen the writing on the wall. They knew it was not going to be a good day. Finally, the head nurse said, "Doctor, it is time to make the call." The doctor looked at the clock, and said, "It's 3:30 P.M., and I pronounce Dexter Hightower to be dead." Those simple words sucked all the air out of the room. One by one, people began to leave the room. The nurses went first. The doctors followed shortly behind them. My body was lying motionless in the hospital bed. The only person left in the room was Coach Rolph. He was still holding my hand. He looked around the room, and said to no one in particular, "You are wrong doctor. Today, Dexter is more alive than ever. Son, I look forward to seeing you soon."

Faith is so powerful. It has the ability to deliver us out of the most difficult circumstances. Faith lifts us up when we think the world has crushed us. It has an amazing way of bringing us hope, when hope seems impossible. It has been said that faith can move mountains. I believe that is a true statement. I have seen faith work in my life, and the lives of the people I love most. Faith has a special way of conquering death and despair. Faith has a way of making us look to the future. Faith brings great vision. Faith has a special way of looking through time. That is always a valuable commodity, when the world seems to be focused on destruction. Faith can be contagious, when it is shared with others. Faith knows no boundaries. Faith is not limited by borders. Faith is colorblind. Faith does not value wealth or poverty. Faith plays no favorites. It has been said that each person has been given a measure of faith. I believe that statement. We all have that measure of faith, in each of our hearts. We have to decide individually, what we will do with that measure of faith. It comes down to being an individual choice. Faith has no children, or grandchildren. May God, continue to grant us the grace to choose wisely. Faith is a special gift from above.

# ABOUT THE AUTHOR

Jerry Hill is the Senior Associate Pastor, at Calvary Chapel Pacific Hills Church. The church is located in Aliso Viejo, California. Jerry also serves as a chaplain, for the Santa Ana Police Department. The police department is located in Santa Ana, California. He has been married to his wife for over 28 years. They have three amazing children. Jerry enjoys golfing, riding his Harley, and Dodgers baseball.

**Twitter: https://twitter.com/jerryhill777**
**Instagram: http://instagram.com/pastorjerryhill**
**Facebook: https://www.facebook.com/pastorjerryhill**

Made in the USA
Lexington, KY
14 August 2019